LITTLE EASTER

by Reed Farrel Coleman

THE PERMANENT PRESS
Sag Harbor, New York 11963

Library of Congress Cataloging-in-Publication Data

Coleman, Reed Farrel, 1956-
    Little Easter / Reed Farrel Coleman.
        p.   cm.
    ISBN 1-57962-139-2 : $18.00
    I. Title.
PS3553.047445L55   1993
813'.54—dc20   92-34305
                                                            CIP

Manufactured in the United States of America.

THE PERMANENT PRESS
4170 Noyac Road
Sag Harbor, NY 11963

For Rosanne and Kaitlin and Dylan Tayor

I would like to thank Tom McDonald for his inspiration and technical advice.

Out of the ash
I rise with my red hair
And I eat men like air.

—Sylvia Plath from "Lady Lazarus"

Johnny Blue

The new TV talked to no one but me. Its virginal speakers babbled to an empty bar, a rapidly decomposing dartboard and a pay-for-pool table at which no one was paying and no one was playing. Taxidermied fishes, with sawdust for souls and glass buttons for eyes, turned deaf ears to the moot squawking, choosing instead to spy threatening harpoons, crossed like dueling foils against the red brick and mortar of the opposing wall. Yes, the new TV talked, but I barely listened. I was too busy blowing imaginary dust out of clean pony glasses and watching the weather.

Sound Hill was wedding dress white, Bing Crosby white, "White Christmas" white. After five fingers worth of years in this town, you'd think I'd be comfortable with the notion of snow keeping its cream for more than a few nods and a wink. I wasn't. Where I come from in Brooklyn, snow falls dirty. At least I remember it that way. Back there the only white snow you see is spray-painted onto shop windows around the holidays. I guess I'm exaggerating, but not much, really. The air's pretty dirty over Brooklyn.

How far was the city; sixty, seventy miles west of here? Yet, for a goodly part of the time, Brooklyn seemed like a distant planet or a place where I came from in someone else's life. I don't know. I talked about it sometimes with my fellow Brooklyn emigré, John Francis MacClough. He didn't know either and cared even less. Like most retired city detectives he'd cracked too many skulls and touched too many corpses to dwell on the metaphysical.

Funny thing about MacClough was that he never much reminded me of that someone else's life or the home planet. No, it took things like white snow to stick its finger down my throat and pull out the past. It took things that kept me off balance, things I'd never adjusted to. Things, I imagine, I hadn't wanted to adjust to. Things that were sort of an escape hatch in case I wanted to travel back and remember. Why I wanted to remember just now, I couldn't say.

Tonight I was in charge of MacClough's lifeless Rusty Scupper, alone with his stiff little fishes and my less than sober thoughts. It was Christmas Eve and I was as comfortable as Moses munching on communion wafers. Forget their protestations to the contrary, all Jews are eternally ill at ease with the whole Christmas ordeal. Hanuka is a nice holiday, but eight colored candles and a four-sided top are no match for the son of God—not even with the points.

When I was a kid, Catholic girlfriends were my remedy for Christmas discomfort. A little turkey, a little midnight mass, a few green and red and white gift-wrapped baubles do wonders for teen-age, Jewish discomfort. Now girlfriends, Catholic or otherwise, were less of a distraction and considerably harder to come by. Since my move to Sound Hill I'd done the volunteer routine, subbing for MacClough on Christmas Eve. It was, after all, the Christian thing to do. Besides, Johnny figured I couldn't do much damage in a predictably empty bar. He'd have never left the Scupper in my hands in July. Twenty years as a beat cop and detective had taught John Francis how to pick his spots.

You see, when the flocks moved east, they moved east in summer. And by no means was the Lord their shepherd. Absolut and orange juice and walk-to beaches with weedy sand dunes like sirens pulled them here. Or was it just the city that pushed them away? It's hard to know for certain, even having lived on both sides of the migration.

Summers in Sound Hill are lovely magnets, but it's spring and winter and fall that make people stay. Things are more real here then. With the passing of Labor Day, life takes on a sort of self-imposed timelessness. The Star Spangled Deli is relieved of its obligation to carry three sizes of French bottled water, six shapes of Japanese rice bran pasta and two brands of Panamanian beer. Over at the service station, Stan Long deflates gas and labor prices back down to a level even people without titles can afford. And the farm stand girls turn in their gingham gowns for cold, early mornings of dirty work and school buses. And . . .

I stopped watching the snow. White weather and alcohol and loneliness are a bad combination, makes a man's mind wonder where maybe it shouldn't. I dug some quarters out of the register, poured myself another Black and Tan and strolled to the pool table for a game of Eight Ball, solitaire style. I set my pint glass down on the edge of the worn and pitted table. I chose the least curved cue from the four sad offerings stuck in the wall rack. Twirling and swooshing the stick with my unskilled hands, I was Cyrano, a samurai, a majorette. One thrust at the elevated TV and the background babbling ended, a powder blue chalkmark on the "Power" switch indicating my success. God, the bar was so awfully quiet now. The cue sliding thru the insides of my fingers was the only sound the world had to offer.

"Is Johnny Blue here?" her emphatic whisper broke the silent spell.

I turned too quickly to the door, carelessly swinging the curved stick and launching the nearly full pint glass into space. Gravity pulled it toward the center of the earth.

"How long have you been standing there?" I knelt in the puddle of ale, stout and glass, more concerned with whether she'd seen my Zorro and baton routine than the presence or absence of one Johnny Blue. Thirty-six-year-old men are vain like that.

"Where is Johnny Blue?" it was less of a whisper this time.

"Look, lady," I came out of my crouch, "that's three questions—two for you and one for me—and we're not gettin' anywhere."

She didn't like that, not that she said so. It was more the way she stiffened under her tattered mink. Her shape was pleasant enough, accented by the soft fur belt pulled in at the waist, but she was no teen-ager. Her overly made-up features were sadly grotesque in that once they must have been neither sad nor grotesque. You could count the mileage in her sleepy, pink-shadowed lids and measure the wear and tear by counting the cracks in her almost orange face powder. I couldn't tell much about what color her hair had been. It'd probably been a lot of colors. Now it was mostly gray and straight and lifeless. Its ends were buried somewhere beneath the half-upturned collar of that once proud coat. Unlike the shattered pint glass, more than carelessness and gravity had contributed to her fall. I could see that even from where I stood.

"Do you mean, MacClough, Johnny MacClough?" I evened up the questions at two apiece, feeling less embarrassed for myself.

"I shouldn't have come," she said to herself, but loud enough for me to catch. Her drained green eyes didn't seem to notice me. "I shouldn't have come."

I started to make my way around the back of the bar. "Sit down a minute and have a—"

"God," she cut my offer of an Irish Coffee short, "I should never have come." And with that she turned on the spikes of her inappropriate black shoes, exiting as quietly as she'd entered.

"Yeah," I said to her fresh memory, "and a merry Christmas to you too!"

That was that. I gave last call. No one objected. No one was there to object. The TV was off, the fishes were dead and my visitor had just departed for parts unknown. I clanged the tip bell a few times for the exercise and came around front of the bar to officially close the Scupper.

"Christ!" I screamed while slipping on the forgotten glass of the cue stick casualty. Unless some wacky guy came in and announced that he was the real Johnny Blue and asked did I know where his mink-coated, orange-faced middle-aged girlfriend had got to, I'd be able to clean up the broken glass in no time. But stepping to the front door, I slipped again. This time I found clear crystals under my shoe that seemed to bear little relation to a broken beer glass.

I dangled the expensive banana peel high above the bar ledge in the soft light of an overhanging globe. The necklace of little cut stones seemed to amplify the dull bar light, breaking it into distinctive sparkling rays. Held close to my amateur's eye, the white gold and diamond confection was alluring and impressive. I counted twenty-four multi-faceted gems aligned like stars in the shape of a heart. Each gem rested in the petrified palm and fingers of petite, but well defined, white gold hands: Twenty-four diamonds, twenty-four little hands. The hands were attached to the heavy heart-shaped body of the setting at the wrists. The orphaned heart appeared unscathed by my clumsy mis-step. Its chain, however, would require a new clasp and some skilled untangling. My best guess was that the heart belonged to Johnny Blue's one-woman fan club.

I threw MacClough's golf sweater on and stepped out into the darkness. If she hadn't come by car, I figured I still had a chance to catch her. Those high spikes of hers would leave a nice easy trail in the snow. Even a former insurance investigator like me could follow footprints like those. At least I told myself I could.

I looked for tire tracks out in front of the Scupper. The surprisingly bitter cold and bitting wind contributed to my disappointment when I didn't find any. My newly revived conscience made me keep on. Her stiletto pumps left a series of triangles and dots in the snow leading toward the Long Island Railroad station. That simplified things a bit. I could check out Carney's Cabs on my way over.

Old man Carney was head back, slack-jawed and dead to the world. His ancient charred lungs silently sucked in huge gulps of chilled air, exhaling the waste gasses with much noisy pomp and circumstance. He held a burning cigarette—now mostly cigarette-shaped ashes—between two yellow fingers resting on the edge of his desk. The tip of the ashen snake lay in a cheap foil ashtray. The smooth split ends of smoke drifted with the currents caused by the old man's wheezing. Orange face wasn't here.

There weren't any more footprints to follow. The sidewalks are shoveled and the streets are plowed this close to the railroad station. Yes, even in Sound Hill. I scanned the passenger platform from the taxi stand's doorway. Both eastbound and westbound looked as empty as Mac-Clough's place, but I decided to walk both sides of the tracks anyway to satisfy a growing curiosity. My very visible breath reminded me that it was pretty damned cold for someone in a bar apron and spring sweater to be playing hide and go seek. Curiosity makes for poor decisions.

The darkness and shadows made it tough to see detail, but I spotted a shaggy tail of dyed mink showing itself from between the clapboard ticketbooth on the westbound platform and a row of four newspaper vending machines which stood shoulder to shoulder against the kiosk's front wall. An icy raw chill shook me; a chill that had nothing to do with cold fronts or Arctic air masses.

I smelled death from across the tracks. The ragged collection of pelts flapped in the wind, but nothing else was moving over there. I stood, arms folded, and stared, waiting for her to fool me. Waiting for her to leap up and come to me demanding the orphaned heart's return and the whereabouts of Johnny Blue. Sweat poured over my back, the frigid air trying to freeze the falling drops between my skin and shirt. The night started closing in, but a distant train horn stopped my swoon. I took small, quick steps across the tracks.

No, she would not fool me nor would she fool anyone ever again. Even before I got to the body, I noticed her leaking blood had stained a patch of slush crimson red. I couldn't help thinking it looked like a fallen cherry snow cone. I was just old enough to remember real snow cones shaved from huge blocks of ice by bald Italian men under the "el" on 86th Street. The only real snow cones you could get in Brooklyn now were in the Black and Puerto Rican neighborhoods.

She was there, face down and to the wall, the back of her ratty coat pressed against the legs of the shoulder-to-shoulder newspaper machines. Almost reflexively, I reached over the vending machines trying to find warmth or a neck pulse. Given the wind chill factor and my lack of gloves, it was a fairly futile gesture. My fingers did find wet, gooey, freezing fur and hair. I pulled the collar down, brushed aside the stiff matted hair and tried to find her throat. The nail and top of my left index finger rubbed up against an earring. I slipped the blind finger beneath her adorned left ear. But instead of finding more flesh, my frozen digit plunged into a moist hole with sharp irregular edges.

Christ! I snatched my arm up with enough momentum to launch it into shallow earth orbit. The cold air caused a clot of the dead woman's blood to roll slowly down the back of my hand like raspberry pancake syrup. Parts of me wanted desperately to be sick. Parts of me wanted to scream my balls off and run and never stop running. But all I could do was gaze at my nearly frostbitten fingertip. It'd touched something in there, in what, I guess, used to be her mouth. It'd touched something that felt like . . . well, like feathers!

I wiped the blood off on my pants and pulled at the squat vending machines. They came away easily, more easily, probably, than they had for the killer. She rolled over. I jumped back, sliding off the low platform onto the tracks. Heavy vibrations told me to get my ass up unless I wanted to become a National Transportation Safety Board statistic. I took the advice and went back to the lady in blood and mink.

She was dead. When I yanked the newspaper machines away, physics rolled her onto her back. My finger *had* touched feathers. The tail end of a yellow downy body and its two frail feet hung out over the woman's blue lips, her too-red lipstick smeared on the lemon-colored feathers of the little bird. Even I knew what the yellow bird symbolized.

She was a rat, a snitch, stooly. She'd turned, rolled over. She'd broken the silence, whispered in the wrong ears, given someone up. She'd testified, turned state's evidence, witnessed for the man. She was a singer, a chanteuse, a canary. That's what the yellow bird meant. It was a mob symbol as time-honored as a tuna in a dead man's tux. The white-hairs drinking grappa and playing bocce in the park used to talk about their crude code. The method of the rub or the condition of the body was usually an allusion to the sin the victim had committed. The mob had funny notions about sins and absolution. But that was in the old days when gangsters wore scars and hats and used words like grifter and gunsel.

A clanging bell and air horn split the silent night as an old diesel locomotive lumbered into Sound Hill station. I paid it almost as little mind as the two dead canaries stiffening by my shoes. The woman's washed-out eyes were open to the cloudy skies. They expressed nothing, not even fear. I wondered about the life-flashing-before-your-eyes cliché and if life was painful in review. It's funny what you think about.

"Hey, buddy," a sour-smelling whiskey voice spoke into my right ear, "Merry Christmas and Peace on Earth." A drunken hand clapped me on the back.

I ignored him.

He didn't much like it. "Ya don't havta be that—" he slurred indignantly. "Oh shit! Holy fuckin' shit! Holy Mary. Oh God! Holy fuckin' shit, man! God! God! What the fuck, man? Christ! Oh God! Holy . . ."

I never caught his face, but I assumed he'd seen the cold mink package on the concrete. I watched him run drunkenly down the platform; sliding and cursing as he went. I was relieved that help would soon be here and happy that someone in this hard world had managed to scream for the dead stranger at my feet.

Mop of Anarchy

I hadn't tasted the apparently hot coffee yet nor could I smell its steam. The cheap porcelain cup rested between my still anesthetized fingers and jittery knees. If the shaking had spilled any of the burning liquid, I couldn't feel it. I rested my dizzy head on the lip of the Scupper's century-old bar. A scratchy Red Cross blanket kept slipping off my shoulders and someone, probably lots of someones, kept putting it back. I liked it better on the floor.

If you were a sucker for men in uniform, the Rusty Scupper was *the* hot spot on eastern Long Island. We had New York State Troopers, Suffolk County cops, Suffolk County Sheriff's deputies, Long Island Railroad cops, Suffolk County Coroner's men, Sound Hill Volunteer Firemen and assorted ambulance drivers from surrounding towns and the forty-eight contiguous United States. I haven't even mentioned the detectives, forensic cops, clergymen and doctors. Oh yeah, old man Carney had snapped out of his catatonia to come have a look see. I'd been to Mets' games less well attended. I half expected a vendor to pop in and start hawking hot dogs and scorecards.

My accounting of this white Christmas was as practiced and polished as any tale ever told. Having presented it to most of the law enforcement officials in the western hemisphere, I'd managed to smooth out any rough edges in my delivery. I even told the truth, mostly. I sort of forgot to mention the fancy cut-glass pendant with the white gold hands. And so what if I told the cops that the

15

dead woman had come into the Scupper to catch her breath from the cold? I just wanted to check with Mac-Clough before telling the truth, the whole truth and nothing but the truth, so help me God. Johnny'd risked his neck for me more than once. I needed to make certain none of this involved him before I conveniently remembered any absent details. I owed him that and more.

And after most of the talking was done, the forensic team took their turn with me. They wanted a swatch of material from all my clothing. I obliged. They asked for MacClough's moth food golf sweater. They needed it to run some nitrate tests. They were sure I hadn't shot the bird lady, but procedure was procedure and they could always get a court order and . . . I gave them the sweater. I told them to keep it. Its replacement was upstairs under Johnny's Christmas tree. They asked for some dried blood from under my fingernail. I let them scrape it. I was in such a giving mood that I volunteered some of my own blood. But that wasn't on their holiday shopping list. Eventually, they withdrew.

From the battalion of volunteer ambulance crews came some freckle-faced kid, with a stethoscope for a necktie, who said he thought somebody ought to have a look at my finger.

"Why?" I wondered.

He hemmed and hawed, mumbling something about small puncture wounds and the dead woman's blood.

"Why?" I repeated.

"AIDS!" he flushed red.

I let him look at the whole hand. He bathed and toweled it and poured what might've been hydrogen peroxide over it to see if any white foam would bubble up. None did. We agreed that testing for leaks in an inner tube was much easier and that I should have a real doctor check it out. He said he'd tell the cops to run an HIV test on the corpse, but that he couldn't guarantee they'd listen. I winked my understanding and thanks. He flushed again and planted the hot coffee in my mitts.

"Mr. Klein?" a throaty woman's voice questioned already knowing the answer.

"Yeah," I spoke not to the woman at my back, but to the cup in my lap.

"I'm Kate Barnum from the *Sound Hill Whaler*."

"Great," I lifted my head off the bar, placing the cheap chinaware in its place. The scratchy blanket slid to the floor again. "Just what I needed, the press."

"Here," the reporter fumbled with the blanket, trying to juggle it with her mini-recorder, pad and pen.

"I prefer it there. Leave it where it lays."

She ceased the juggling act and let go of the woolen blanket.

Unlike the dead woman, Kate Barnum had never been pretty. Guys would call her interesting, just interesting, eternally interesting. I liked interesting. Interesting usually had more depth than flat out pretty and certainly more than beautiful. Her dull blond hair was a curly mop of anarchy; tight ringlets here, droopy twirls there. Her brows were brown and thick in opposition to thin, pale lips and an incongruously delicate nose. Her skin was blotchy from stress and Scotch and cigarettes. And the weak make-up job couldn't hide where her cheeks sagged slightly at the flanks of her square chin and under crystal gray eyes. Without those eyes she'd be less interesting, but that was one factor we didn't have to worry about.

"Now that your sharp eyes have surmised I'm not the reincarnation of Marilyn Monroe, can I ask you some questions about this evenings events?"

I thought about denying the dual correctness of her assessment, but chose instead to hold her inquiries at arm's length.

"Are you always so charmingly egocentric?" I wondered.

"Sorry," she gave an insincere bow. "It's just a line I learned at a Carnegie seminar. Helps break the ice at parties. I do so hate making small talk."

"Me too; small talk, big talk, any kinda talk. I've talked myself sore. So let's skip it."

"Come on, Mr. Klein, give us both a break," the blue-jeaned and cowboy-booted Barnum was suddenly more sincere. "It's late. I'm tired. You're tired . . ."

"You forgot to mention it's Christmas Day," I scolded. She plopped her mini-recorder unceremoniously on the bar and rolled up the ends of her frayed sweater sleeves. "It's Christmas Day. It's late. I'm tired. You're tired . . . There! Is that any better?"

"Kate Barnum. Kate Barnum," I repeated in a loud whisper, ignoring her question. "I know that name. I've read it somewhere."

"In the *Whaler,*" she tried to deflect my meanderings.

"No . . ." I drifted on, running pages of old newsprint from memory past my internal eye. As an insurance investigator, I'd had plenty of dead time for reading the papers. "*The New York Times.* That's it!" I slapped the bar in self-satisfaction, landing my hand uncomfortably close to her Sony. "You slummin'?"

"Not slumming, Mr. Klein."

"You've fallen quite a ways from the *Times.*"

"Farther than you can ever know," Kate Barnum's face took on a sadly serene glow like a leper at peace with her fate.

I'd had to talk to the cops. Even Bojangles himself couldn't've tapped his way around that. Reporters were different. Why say anything to anyone anyway, until I hooked up with John Francis in the morning? A prudent man would've followed MacClough's Law: *Never speak to the fucking press. They can't twist what you don't say, though they try hard enough.* But Johnny was an ex-cop and cops rated the press third on their shit list just behind politicians and criminal lawyers and ahead of serial killers and child molesters.

I spoke to her. Maybe just because she had fallen. For me, that could be enough. Interesting and fallen, my kind of woman. But I'd have to explore that weakness of mine some other night. For now I dusted off and trotted out the same old version of the night's happenings that I'd spoon-fed the law. They'd seemed satisfied with it. I figured it would make Barnum happy, too. That was my mistake.

"Look, Mr. Klein," the reporter smirked, shaking her head like a skeptical teacher listening to an excuse about a pit bull eating his master's homework. "Even if I bought the coincidence of Jane Doe just popping in out of nowhere to catch her breath, I couldn't swallow the rest of it with a five-pound bag of sugar. It doesn't hang together. Like why did you follow a complete stranger out into the cold and snow while leaving the bar totally unattended? You see what I mean?"

"I was concerned about her," I tried meekly. "She seemed a little unbalanced. I don't know."

"Okay, then, why didn't you go after her immediately or try and stop her from leaving at all? No, Mr. Klein. I may have tumbled a long distance from the city beat at the *Times*, but I didn't have a lobotomy on the way down."

"The cops liked—"

"The cops!" she threw up her hands. "The cops wanted to get home for the holiday."

I surveyed the Scupper. It *had* pretty much emptied out. This wasn't the crime scene, after all. And they'd pretty much finished with me.

"The cops," Barnum started up again. "Just because they're pretty sure you didn't kill the stiff, doesn't mean they believed you. Cops work slowly, but don't mistake that for stupidity. They can afford to come back tomorrow and tomorrow and tomorrow."

I knew she was right, but I only needed one tomorrow. I was stalling for a ten-minute chat with MacClough.

"You asked for the story," I put on an angry mask. "You got the story. Life's weird sometimes. Sometimes things don't hang together. Like promising careers, for instance."

I might just as well have stabbed her for the pain on her face. No, I don't think a knife would've hurt quite so much. But she refused to take up the mask of anger. In fact, she didn't do anything but shrink.

"Can I buy a drink?" she wanted to know, tensely biting down on her bottom lip. The interview was over. "Bourbon?"

"Sure," I got up off the stool and made my way behind the bar.

The last of the occupying armada "Merry Christmased" their way out the door. One or two of the detectives suggested I not do any interstate visiting any time soon. I explained that I hated holiday travel anyway.

"Wild Turkey or Maker's Mark?" I refocused on the thirsty reporter.

"Haven't you got anything cheaper?" she wondered, throwing some balls of crumpled currency onto the bar top.

"Don't sweat it," I flicked the crushed bills back to her. "Tonight it's on the house. You can pay for the speed rack bourbon next trip."

If I'd been expecting any proud protests, they weren't forthcoming.

"Maker's Mark," was all she had to say.

"On the rocks or—"

"—straight," Barnum stole the second option from my throat. "Straight. Neat. A double. And now," she rattled off like some throwaway character of Hemingway's.

She didn't bother trying to coax me into joining her. Kate Barnum no longer cared about drinking alone. Three double bourbons' worth of watching showed me she'd gotten over that hump some time ago. I poured her a fourth before putting the long-necked bottle dressed in fake, drippy-red wax back on the shelf over my shoulder.

"I smell a good story here, Klein," she tried that bit of triteness on for size.

"That's your breath you're smellin', Ms. Barnum. Now why don't you go home and write it up like I explained?"

"Because your telling stinks worse than my breath," she slammed the evacuated tumbler onto the pitted counter and lit up a filterless Chesterfield. A few drinks and the first drag on her cigarette seemed to put some wind back in her sails. "You don't fool me, Klein. I'm going to get this story. It wants me to get it."

"There's no story to get."

"You're right," she agreed too easily. "When a middle-aged woman dressed in Salvation Army mink and made up like an orange day-glo hooker gets her brains re-arranged and a canary stuffed in her dead mouth in this town, that's not a story. That's legend, my friend."

With that pronouncement, she swept her collection of crushed dollar bills off the bar and into a hip pocket. She threw on a ski parka that'd probably never seen the slopes nor the insides of a dry cleaners. The beige coat was so worn and soiled you could divine the outlines of where the tape recorder was usually carried. And that's the pocket she put it in.

"Save your Merry Christmases for someone who'll listen," the thoroughly braced reporter preempted, waving her right palm at me like a poor man's Diana Ross. Kate Barnum was a veteran drinker. The straight, stumble-free line she made out of the bar proved as much. She didn't have to tell me I'd be seeing her again. I knew I would. Parts of me looked forward to it. Still others smelled trouble in the wake of her perfume. I finally locked the Scupper's front doors. Some of me wanted to collapse into sleep, but that was for books and movies and my three wishes. I tended to wear insomnia like a second skin. I shut the bar lights, settled down with the stuffed fishes and let the new TV babble once again.

Jacob Marley, wrapped in chains and moaning—sort of like my brother Josh getting his cavities drilled by Great Uncle "Who Needs Novacaine" Ziggy, in Brighton Beach in 1963—was busily laying guilt at the feet of old Scrooge. Ebenezer wasn't having any, yet. He had three ghosts to go. I dangled the orphaned heart in the TV glare and wondered how many ghosts might be waiting to visit the likes of one John Francis MacClough.

Diary of Wasted Days

My right arm was warmly numb underneath her. The smooth inside of my left forearm could feel the soft ridges of branching blue veins buried just beneath the cloudy white skin of her breasts. Curling my left wrist with eager pain, I captured a bullet-hard nipple between the tips of my thumb and forefinger. I pinched the pink bullet and she shook. Suddenly, something else stiffened, something resting between the pillow of her buttocks and the moist opening of her soul.

She released her nipple from my grip and guided my fingers south along her abdomen, over the lightly downed skin below her waist and into a wet tangle of hair and hunger. My fintertip chased and caught an elusive button hidden under the coarse weave and slippery skin. I dipped my finger fully into her and brought the moisture to my mouth.

God, she was different. My finger smelled of patchouli and she tasted like bourbon and cigarettes on my tongue. I could feel my thighs tighten as a drop of me rolled onto her somewhere. She grabbed my hand and licked it, too.

"You don't fool me, Klein," her throaty whisper faded into the black.

I rolled her over to kiss her, to cut my tongue on her teeth. My hands cupped her cheeks and I pressed down on her. I never reached her lips.

Feathers and brittle claws!

We lay together on the train platform. Her eyes still vacantly searching the arc-lighted sky. There was blood, again, on the end of my finger, on my lips and rolling onto the snow from the tip of my penis.

I tried running, but my naked feet were tractionless against the frozen concrete and ice. I slid every second step, peeling my skin away in sheets. There was no pain nor much blood.

At the edge of the station, a dark form pulled me up. It was bound and shackled and wore a diamond heart at the end of a stethoscope.

"Your hands." It grabbed them. "I want your hands. They want me to get them."

The shadow man squeezed my hands. I could feel that more clearly, now, and the sweat consuming what was left of my unpeeled skin.

"Hey, Klein!" he shook my shoulders. "Klein!" a rough hand slapped my cheeks. "For chrissakes!"

My shoulders were free. A chair crashed. So did I.

"I thought a fall on that flat Jewish ass might wake you up." Johnny MacClough stood over me shaking his head in mock disgust. "Must've been a helluva dream."

"That," I yawned, cracking my stiff neck, "was no dream."

The cloud-filtered morning light seemed to bend around MacClough on its journey to my crusty eyes. I rubbed them to no good end and began scratching at the ever-increasing gray of my beard. Why was it, I wondered, that gray hair looked so distinguished on everyone else. On me it looked like a diary of wasted days. On me it was a constant reminder of knees that stayed sore too long and breath that just grew shorter. It's funny what you wonder about.

Johnny MacClough had no beard nor any gray hair in his full blond waves. Though a good ten years my senior, he'd always introduce me to people as his father. As yet, no one was quite blind enough to believe it, but sometimes, just sometimes, strangers hesitated a bit too long before laughing.

"Merry Christmas!" I threw my right hand out for a shake and a pull up.

"Bar looks like shit," he observed accusingly, but yanked me up just the same.

"You heard?" I rolled my shoulders and stretched.

"I heard. Carney practically jumped me on my way in. I haven't seen the old bastard that agitated since they cut out his right lung. He was a little sketchy on the details, but your name kinda got mentioned every third word."

"Yeah, it was quite a party."

"Do tell," Johnny sat down at the bar where Kate Barnum had sat. "Do tell."

I did. I told. Everything, this time. He wore his cop face, absorbing it all like a skeptical sponge. I hated that particular face, that cop face. The face that saw only enemies. The face that says: "Yeah, right! You lying scumbag. Stop wasting my time and tell me the truth. Truth? I wouldn't believe it anyway coming outta your mouth." I hated that face because it was reflexive and showed a MacClough I didn't know, couldn't know, didn't want to know. I told myself he couldn't help it. That attitudes couldn't be left at the door like service revolvers and badges. But I still hated that face.

"Johnny Blue, huh?" the ex-detective peeled off the cynical make-up sooner than expected, almost too soon. "Good name for a rockabilly star."

"So you're not—"

"—Johnny Blue. No. Sorry to disappoint you."

"And this doesn't mean anything to you?" I fished the diamond heart out of my pocket.

"Not unless it means we're goin' steady," he gave a

cursory glance at the orphaned heart. "Thanks, Dylan," he never called me that.

"For . . ."

"For putting on the stall until we talked. Merry Christmas ya heathen Jew bastard." He hugged me.

"You're welcome, but now how do I tell the cops about these new details? I wasn't shocky or anything. It's gonna look pretty suspicious."

"Here," Johnny snatched the jewlry out of my paw. "I'll handle it."

"But—"

"But nothin'. I said I'll deal with it and I will. I do the cop-speak thing pretty damned well," he bragged, sounding more like the man I knew.

"So whaddaya think?" I tried turning the page back to the subject of murder.

"About what?" MacClough wanted to know, sniffing at the cold coffee I'd left on the bar the night before.

"About raggy mink ladies with orange make-up. About little yellow birds and bullet holes. About—"

"Where's my sweater," John cut me off.

"The cops. I told you. Nitrate tests. Remember?"

"Yeah," he waved carelessly. "I never believed half the shit those forensic guys came up with. I swear they used to make their results up as they went along."

"What about the murder?" I refused to let go.

"What about it? Murder is murder. When you strip away all the frills, all you got is a dead human being," was the ex-cop's strangely undetective-like conclusion. "The bird? Could be window dressing. Could be it just flew into her mouth. Maybe Frank Perdue is a serial killer. I don't know. It's fuckin' Christmas Day. Can we get off the subject?"

"Sure," I gave in uneasily. "Let's clean up."

"No, not today. I'll do it tomorrow." He squeezed the

back of my neck with brotherly affection. "Let's go open some gifts."

"Okay, MacClough," I shook his calloused right hand.

He took one long look at the barroom and stood, head bowed, for some seconds. It seemed oddly like a moment of prayer.

London in December

Whenever I could not write, I'd assemble mental lists of authors and poets I could barely approximate and never be. There were very many lists. I would never be F. Scott or J.R.R. or e.e. or T.S. or J.D. or W.H. or D.H. or H.D. I'd never be Ernest or Ezra, Wallace or William, Kurt or Carlos, Richard or Raymond, Ann, Anne, or Ayn. I would never be Leo or Isaac, Hammett or Hesse, T. Wolfe or V. Woolf. I *would* always be Dylan, but neither Bob nor Thomas.

I was furiously making lists today. I was making lists to camouflage the bald spot on my brain where the words had stopped coming from. I was making lists to distract my eyes from the mounting pile of crumpled white paper surrounding my desk like unmelting snowballs. I was making lists to ease the frustration of blank pages. Blank pages; the only thing that ever made insurance work seem like romance.

When the lists didn't work, I'd read. I was reading today. I was reading my own stuff; the three poems and two short stories that'd been published since my change of career. Sometimes reading my own printed words would pump me up, slap me, throw cold water in my face, fool me into believing there was hope and promise in the world and within me. Today, I wasn't fooling so easy. Early on, I tried to juice myself by staring at photostats of the publishers' payment checks, but today their sparse digits only fueled the frustration.

I switched to the product of someone else's pen. I picked

29

up the *Whaler* and studied something other than the grocery ads for the first time in five years. God, she really *was* good. Her sentences were as clean and taut as an old sailor's knots. Her skepticism was sharp, but veiled like the microscopic teeth on a scalpel. Didn't you know? All knives have teeth. All knives. She had knives. She had teeth. She knew how to use them. Again the question came. What had she done to fall this far?

Yeah, I'd pulled Kate Barnum's name out of my memory's hat. Her prose, however, had not been so readily retrievable. I guess I didn't really have much respect for tabloid journalism. To me, newspaper writing was like newspaper print; easily washed off, easily forgotten. It really was some feat, you know, my recalling her name. Considering a good part of my newspaper reading had been done between sips of burned-bitter coffee in dull, heaterless front seats during eternal nights of mostly fruitless surveillance, it's a wonder I could remember my own name. Then another question arose. Why did I remember hers?

The phone clicked or buzzed or whatever it was that phones did now in the digital age. I let its chips exercise their synthesized lungs until another wonder of the age threw its robotic two cents in.

"Hi! I'm not in right now," my recorded voice lied, "or I'm listening to make sure I'm in the mood to speak to you." That was more like it. "In any case, leave your name, number and time you called. I'll try to get back to you soon as possible. 'Bye."

"Mr. Klein, this is Kate Barnum. If you're there, please pick up. . ." she waited. I waited. "Okay, then," she went on, "I'd like to apologize for my behavior at the bar the other night. God, I'm sounding like such a jerk." There was real discomfort in that pronouncement and it was followed by real anger. "I hate these fucking machines. If I could go back in time, I'd go back and kill the bastard who invented them."

"Not me," I picked up, interrupting her vengeful ramblings. "I'd go back and kill Van McCoy."

"Van McCoy?"

"Van McCoy. You remember. 'Do the hustle, doo doodoo doo doo doodoo doo doo. . .' I hated fuckin' disco music," I was actually gritting my teeth.

"Oh, him. He's already dead," Barnum delivered the good news.

"Hey, the guy who invented phone machines is also probably dead," I chimed in sarcastically.

"Yeah, it sure is a wonderful life."

"Ain't it grand, though," I paused. "I know there's a point here somewhere and don't tell me you really called to apologize."

"It gave me a convenient opening," she admitted easily enough.

"To. . ." I wondered.

"To invite you to dinner tonight."

I answered with silence. The kind of silence heavier than spent uranium wrapped in lead. The kind of silence louder than sonic booms in the Grand Canyon. She understood.

"No," she replied to the unspoken questions, "my motives aren't purely social. And yes, I'll probably ask about the dead woman and your lame story concerning the events surrounding her demise. Look," she cleared her throat, "I was a bit of an ass the other night—"

"A bit," I agreed.

"Thanks for making this so easy," Barnum replied sarcastically.

"Think nothin' of it."

"Will you shut up, please!" There was strain, all right. "You know you aren't half bad looking for a guy as gray as London in December. And if you really are the man who wrote this dark poem I just finished reading," she ruffled some pages by her phone's mouthpiece, "then we should be able to get through dinner without much bloodletting. Even if you don't answer my inevitable questions. What do you say?"

"I say you're tryin' too hard," I paused a few beats, "but it's been a long time since anyone's tried at all. So, yeah, sure. I'm game."

"My digs. Eight, eight-thirty."

The rest of the conversation consisted of directional babble: "Make a sharp left after the alley behind Smythe's Antique's . . ." That sort of thing. Sound Hill didn't really have a wrong side of the tracks, but her address was located in that part of town which came closest to qualifying.

I had neglected to ask what we were having for dinner. I guess I really wasn't very interested. I was, however, very interested in her. I felt it in my head and in my pants. From her fall to my poetry to her apology, she had pushed every right button there was to push. I forgot about attempting to write or making long lists. What I did do was to recall, in detail, the nightmare I'd had on the evening of the yellowbird murder and to try and regain the feeling of Kate Barnum's imagined breasts in my now curious hands.

Cat Sneeze

The Christmas lights were not so bright here. Residents of Dugan's Dump were no less religious than other Sound Hillians. They just tended to be lower on the great American scale of the middle class. Besides, pronking reindeer with synchronous flashing antlers would have looked incongruous amongst the wilting wooden bungalows. Dirt was the major feature of Dugan's Dump; dirt lawns and dirt driveways. And in every third yard the rotting hulks of lobster boats and Edsels waited patiently on cinder blocks and bent rims for the pick-axes of future archeologists. But the wanna-be artifacts that decorated this part of town had nothing to do with its appellation, at least not originally.

All of the Christmas Eve snow was gone; some back to the clouds, most back to the soil. Around here, that was trouble. And when I pulled off the pavement of Owl Lane, the reporter's driveway started swallowing the tires on my old Volkswagen. But if fifteen-odd years of my driving hadn't killed the clutch, this surely wouldn't. That's what I told myself. That's always what I told myself.

There were no shipwrecks or encrusted cars in Kate Barnum's front yard, just a lone dead apple tree and a corrugated garage waiting for a cat sneeze to blow it over. Her bungalow was a match for most of the others on surrounding plots; sturdy, but unspectacular. I followed the cracked flagstones to her door.

She was waiting for me in the vacated jamb, shaking her head and blowing streams of smoke through cracks in a cynical smile. The sleeves of her gray Yale jersey formed lumpy bundles above her calloused elbows. The collar of the ashen sweatshirt was slit into a V-shape and, intentionally or not, it accented the braless cleavage underneath. Her jeans were scratchy new and hid the necks of cowboy boots I'd seen once before. As I was about to take the singular step up to Kate's pedestal, she flicked her cigarette into the night and kissed me.

It was a rough, tongueless kiss. We both kept wary eyes open and let the kiss die without any attempts to prolong it or move onto other things. I could taste her tobacco in my mouth. No bourbon, yet. It was more a message, I thought, than a kiss. I just had to learn the code.

I stepped up. She waved me in. The front door slammed. My eyes were immediately captured by the network of hand-hewn timber beams crossing above us and rising up to the roof. The walls and floors were an amalgam of broad planks, pitted, bowed and dark with years. She followed my eyes.

"I guess you didn't know. That's why they call this Dugan's Dump," my hostess explained.

"What?" I turned toward the crackling flames and disintegrating logs in the stone fireplace.

"They're ships' masts, carrying beams and parts of their decks and hulls. All the shacks in 'The Dump' are what's left of Conrad Dugan's whaling fleet. Here," she threw back the frilled corner of a faded indigo rug that lay at the foot of the fireplace. Carved deeply into one of the wide floor boards were scrolled capital letters spelling, 'THE DRAGON QUEEN.'

"Conrad Dugan," Kate Barnum shook her head, "that stubborn old bastard. He ran Sound Hill in the whaling days. More than ten of my family manned his ships. Three drowned in the Atlantic while sailing this one," she dragged her booted foot across the name carved into the flooring.

"How'd his ships end up out here?" I had a flare for predictable questions.

"When the whaling industry started its decline, Dugan's advisers told him to sell off his fleet. Take the money and run. But like I said, Dugan was a stubborn old coot and refused. Seems he got this idea to turn Sound Hill into a combination Coney Island/Mystic Seaport type of affair. Really ahead of his time, if you consider it," the reporter paused and considered.

"Well, the old guy figures the tourists would get a real charge out of staying in hotels built out of his old ships. He owned all the land around here. So he had his fleet sailed into Kaitlin Cove and hauled overland the rest of the way. Kind of tough dragging ships through dense woods."

"That's why there's so much dirt!" I blurted out as if I'd stumbled onto the secret of time travel. "He had all the trees chopped down."

"Right," she gave a condescending wink. "That old tree out front came after the slaughter."

"Sounds like an expensive proposition, all that chopping and hauling."

"Bankrupted the old prick," she lit another cigarette. "Coney Whale Land never had a chance."

"But there was all this cleared land and the vessels were already on site."

"Right again, Klein," she flicked ashes into the fire. "The town fathers, in conjunction with Dugan's creditors, had a mini Oklahoma land rush of sorts. For a fifty-dollar fee, any Dugan employee could receive a plot of land out here. The only condition was that the employee had to build a substantial dwelling on the land within two months."

"Hence, Dugan's Dump." Satisfied with my inductive powers, I threw my flat ass onto a wicker sofa.

"Don't get so cozy," Barnum admonished. "We've got to go pick up dinner. I hope you like pizza."

"Haven't found any out here that compares with the city."

"Yeah, I know, but you'll like it better than my cooking. Come on," she pulled me up and threw on that unclean ski jacket. "This place in Floyd's Bend is pretty good. Besides, the walk will build up your appetite."

"Walk!" I stepped back. "My appetite's just fine. Floyd's Bend is five miles from—"

"Two miles and I know a shortcut. Please."

"Fine. Fine," I relented grudgingly.

She kissed me again. This time it was soft and close-eyed and encouraging. "Thanks, Klein," she opened the door. "Walking helps curb my thirst and I don't want to drink around you. Not tonight, anyhow."

The walking wasn't bad, especially when we stuck to the blacktop. Kate Barnum surprised me with her relative silence. Oh, every now and then my guide would point out odd features of "The Dump." There were the vaguely visible ruts the wheels of ship transports had left. She showed me where two of the bungalows had ship names still showing on outer walls. We even passed a shack Jackson Pollack had rented for awhile before heading farther east.

"Swede Thorson, the landlord, tossed Pollack out on his ass for ruining the floors. Dumb schmuck had the floors sanded and refinished," Barnum put on a face of sad resignation and shook it. "Not much good comes out of 'The Dump' and stays out. Any good gets sucked right back in. It's like our own little Dain Curse."

I took that last bit of proud self-pity as a reference to her fall. I'd have to ask her about that fall. And speaking of asking; she wasn't doing any. That didn't fit. I'd pretty much figured this little trek of ours was a ploy on her part to get me alone, off balance and on unfamiliar ground. Lord knows, when we finally turned off the paved portion of our route, the ground became very unfamiliar. I waited for questions about the Christmas killing, about what had really been spoken between the dead Jane Doe and myself. My wait was in vain.

We were almost out of Dugan's Dump, some fifty yards from the tree line that marked the edges of Floyd's Bend when my guide took another fall.

"Shit!" she propped herself up, wiping her muddied palms against one another. "Goddamit," she scowled back at the stone or wind-blown tree limb that had tripped her.

It was a limb, all right; a human limb. Like a deformed sapling, a very wet, very stiff, very dead man's hand thrust itself up through the moist soil at the outskirts of Dugan's Dump. Even in the dark night we could make out the form of the sapling's hastily buried roots. I couldn't help thinking of the dead apple tree in Kate Barnum's yard.

The reporter's momentum had snapped the hairy, white hand back at the wrist. It hung palm up now, fingers clamped as if to grasp. But all it held were some crumbs of mud and some cool air. One of the dead sapling's branches wore a gold and onyx pinky ring. Already I didn't like him.

"The shooter," Barnum and I spoke simultaneously.

"Yeah, I bet there's a gun buried around here too."

She shook her head in agreement: "And I bet you it matches the one that killed your mink-coated lady friend with the mouth full of feathers."

"Let's get to a phone," I started back to the landlocked Dragon Queen.

"No!" she nearly tackled me. 'We can't call this in."

"Maybe *we* can't," I shrugged off her considerable grip, "but I sure as hell can."

"Wait, goddamit. Just hear me out."

I kept walking. She ran past me. Stopped. Grabbed my coat collar, tangled her arms with mine and spun her buttocks into my lower groin. I was up over her back, then in the air, then on my back in the mud. I didn't slap the ground in time to break my fall and my sore, deflated lungs punished me for that sin.

"Are you okay?" my judo instructor, kneeling over me, was keen to know.

"Fuck you," I wheezed out without much force, but lots of conviction.

"I had to get you to listen before you did anything we both might regret." She propped me up.

"Look lady," I was almost breathing now, "I don't exactly know what your game is, but I'm not as dumb as I must seem." I tried to stand and quickly stopped trying. "You wanted me to find that stiff." I pointed at the petrified hand. "You knew right where it was."

"I did," Barnum admitted matter-of-factly. "I found it yesterday, Christmas Day."

"And you didn't call the cops?"

"Hey, if they were too lazy to look, why should I help 'em?" she answered unconvincingly. "The cops should have been all over this place like stink on shit."

"Nice turn of a phrase," I got up and stayed up. "But the law's laissez-faire attitude doesn't explain away your curious, not to mention, illegal behavior."

"Look at me, Klein," she screamed, pulling my face to hers. "Take a close look. I'm a forty-one-year-old alcoholic. I've got no kids. I've got two broken marriages and a broken career to my credit. I don't know if I can stop drinking. I'm not getting any younger, so kids are out. Which is bully for them. One of my marriages turned out to be six months of mutual disdain and the other ended in suicide. The only thing I've got that's fixable, that's worth fixing, that I need to fix, is my career," Kate Barnum was crying mascara-black tears.

"Yeah, and so . . ." I dropped off, not understanding the connection between her misfortune and failure to alert the local constabulary.

"God, Klein," she wiped her ebony tear tracks, smearing them and adding forgotten mud. "Maybe you are that dumb. If I called in the law, I'd be out. You can't

write the story and be part of it. Even little town newspapers have their ethical standards." Those last two words
stuck in her throat like an open tube of Krazy Glue. "Ex-
iled out here, I'm not going to get too many stories that
can help salvage my career. I've got to have this story."

"All right, I've been in tight spots. I'll call it in and keep
your name out of it."

"Do you think I went through all the machinations of
getting you out here just so you could do something I
could've done anonymously twenty-four hours ago?" She
didn't wait for an answer. "No sir. I've got a connection
at *Newsday* who's willing to take a chance on me if I can
deliver a special story all wrapped up like a Christmas
present. This is the story. You're going to solve it. I'm
going to write it. And then I am going back to the top."

"Lady, I'm not solving anything and the only place
you're goin' is to Pilgrim State Psychiatric. Maybe I buy
your hearts and flowers about how your life's been a big
bag of shit lately, but don't try to bury me in it. Like I
said, I'll keep your name out of it." I was walking again.
She did not follow.

"Johnny MacClough," she whispered at my back.

My spine went suddenly cold. The cold slowed me
down, made me hesitate. She was bluffing again, grasping
at straws. But was she? I stopped.

"Yeah," I turned around, "what about him?"

"Johnny MacClough," louder this time, "Johnny Mac-
Clough," louder, "Johnny MacClough," louder still. She
cackled like a B-movie witch pleased by the results of her
incantations.

"Look," I grabbed her shoulders and shook, "this ain't
Shakespeare, baby. This is murder. So fuck you and fuck
your precious career." I collected her colorless hair in my
left hand and yanked her head back. "Stop trying to throw
parties for people who aren't interested in coming. Leave
Johnny out of this."

"Too late," Barnum smiled up at me, shaking her hair out of my loosened grip. "He's already in it. He's in deeper than Mr. Pinky Ring."

"How?"

"No, Klein," she stepped back, rubbing her shoulders. "I don't think so."

"Ah," I shook my spinning head at her, "you're bluffing!"

"Am I? Then go call the law," she flapped her hands at me as if shooing off an annoying fly. "Go call the cops. He's your friend, baby," she mocked me, "not mine."

I left her, but the chill followed. She had my attention and she knew it. I wasn't about to call the cops until I did some checking of my own. She was right. Johnny was *my* friend, maybe the best I ever had. I told myself he had no part in this, that she was throwing his name out in desperation. But the knot in my guts called me a liar. Johnny was involved. I knew it. No, I felt it.

When I was almost back to the paved road, Kate Barnum called after me: "You know my number, Klein." I kept walking. "Don't forget how to dial it."

The hike back to my car took a few minutes less than forever. My knees were sore and my head pounded in rhythm with my heart. My stomach was full of nothing. I needed to sit. I did, on the front fender of my old VW. That, like most other things I'd ever done, was a mistake. My added two hundred pounds forced the ancient bug's tires deep into the driveway's mud. Now, I thought, there were at least two things other than scavenged ships buried in the soil of Dugan's Dump.

Desperate Seed

I needed a drink; a particular drink from a certain bartender.

The Rusty Scupper was busy for Christmas week. Beside the usual crowd, two incongruous Japanese men in pin strikes were furiously waving Scotch-full tumblers at selections on the jukebox and exclaiming over loudly at one another. You didn't have to be an expert in languages of the Pacific rim to divine that one wanted to hear Little Richard and the other, Elvis. Until they resolved their dispute, we'd all hear nothing but them.

Stan Long, the gas station owner, gave me a vaguely drunken nod and went back to cleaning the grease that would never come out from under his nails. No one else turned cartwheels for me. No one ever did. I was hoping to get to the bar without MacClough's recognition. Life would be more simple without hope. Before I'd taken my third step, Johnny was busy tapping a Black and Tan. My drink. A drink I never needed to order here.

My head was swimming. No, drowning. Mistrusting MacClough hadn't really occurred to me before. It occurred to me now. I thought John Francis was a lot of things, but never a murderer. Maybe! Everyone has closets and old bones in them. Some skeletons take a long time to rattle. I guess some never do. I tried telling myself it was just a desperate seed Kate Barnum had planted and that it would never flower. But when you are trying to convince yourself, you've already lost.

"Hey," Johnny slapped the stout and ale on the bar, "it's the wandering Jew from Brighton Beach."

I put my right palm in his and we shook them a few times.

"What's wrong?" he wanted to know.

I took too big of a swallow and nearly spit it up through my nose onto the bar. "Nothing," I coughed. "Are ya takin' up palm readin'?"

"Not if they're all as sweaty as yours. God!" Mac-Clough rubbed his hands on his apron for emphasis.

"Sorry," I took a more human gulp. "What are they doin' here?" I pointed at the Japanese contingent in an attempt to change subjects.

"Don't know," the barman shrugged his shoulders, "maybe they wanna build a golf course in Dugan's Dump."

I managed to laugh. "Tutti Fruiti" was now blasting on the box. Little Richard had won. I turned to the Japanese to wink my approval, but they were too busy mouthing the words and playing air piano.

"So . . ." the ex-cop paused, "what's wrong?"

"Nothing. I don't know. The Christmas blues, I guess."

"You're Jewish."

"Exactly." I put my empty glass up for another pour. "You ever get around to having that chat with the Suffolk cops?" I dropped the question in as skillfully as an armless man threading a needle.

Johnny gave me a killing glance: "In the city we were cops. Out here they're overpaid meter maids with handguns."

"Well?" I persisted.

"Well what?" he put down my refilled glass. "Yeah," MacClough recalled the issue at hand almost wistfully, "it's all talked out. What are you so interested for, anyway?"

"Hey," I attacked in a whsiper. "I was the one who lied to the cops. I was the one who found the diamond heart.

I was the one who found the body. Your fucking sweater was as close as you got to any of it."

"Calm down," he reached across the bar and smacked my cheek affectionately. "I surrender. You got plenty of right to be curious. To the Irish," the ex-detective shouted over Little Richard, raising a Bushmill's to the startled Japanese, "and those who wish they could be."

The two little pinstriped men bowed slightly from the waist, poured a few fingers worth of amber off their own drinks and began arguing over the next jukebox number. Stan Long threw a greasy buck on the bar, muttered something about Guadalcanal and nodded his scornful *adieus*. Bob Street, from the Star Spangled Deli, replaced Stan at the bar.

"Tall Bud, please. What's eating Stan?" Bob wanted to know.

As if choreographed, both MacClough and I threw pointing fingers at the jukebox and harmonized: "They're building a golf course in Dugan's Dump."

John and I waited just long enough for the neon dollar signs to flash in Bob's eyes before we started laughing. I slapped Bob's back and MacClough roughed the deliman's hair.

"The two jokers from Brooklyn." Street finished the rest of his beer in silence with a scowl.

To make amends, I bought Bob another Bud. And in the name of global understanding, I sent a round over to the Nipponese duet by the Wurlitzer. They sent two rounds back. This sparked MacClough's competitive nature and he bought everyone a shot on the house. Things quickly degenerated into an Olympic drinking event. Everybody would bring home the gold tonight, but we'd all be trading in our medals for aspirin in the morning.

Following a serious bout of bowing, back slapping, winking and hand pumping, I stood with Sato and Tadamichi. There was no golf course in their futures nor in ours. No, they'd just wanted to visit an old American whaling village before returning to their jobs as executives in the commercial fishing industry. Too bad Conrad Dugan wasn't around to exploit their apparent fascination. After the introductions, we wound up bleating "Suspicious Minds" along with Elvis. God, we were awful, but it felt awfully good.

Kate Barnum's ruse *had* been a desperate seed. After laughing with John Francis, I was sure of it. I felt it, or maybe that was simply the alcohol. I don't know. Maybe in her shoes I would've tried the same stunt. I wasn't anxious to find out any time soon. I was free of the witch's curse and the world was a better place off my shoulders.

I said my "see ya laters" to Bob and Johnny and did some ceremonial partings with the fishermen in suits. I had to get home. I felt like writing. That lasted until I reached my car door. By then the only thing I felt like doing was throwing up. And not being into self-denial, I did exactly that.

Buddha Belly

I never did get around to writing that night nor did I find the words to report the dead sapling buried in the mud of Dugan's Dump. I did, however, manage to have one hell of a hangover.

A week had come between the world and me and that hangover. I was ten pages into a short story about two Japanese businessmen and a small town's reaction to their visit. I suppose I was trying to say something about stereotypes and judging books . . . You know. But really, I was just having fun playing with words.

In Sound Hill, most of the talk had turned from the murdered woman and her pet canary to returned Christmas ties and already broken New Year's resolutions. Even Kate Barnum had seemed to let it go. Her works in the *Whaler* focused mostly on pork barrel bills before the county legislature.

Oh yeah, I still hadn't summoned up the will to call the cops. For all I knew, the dead man was still out there rotting in the barren field. I make no excuses for my procrastination. I didn't want to stir things up or rattle anyone's cage. Sleeping dogs were going to lie right where they were. For all my confidence in MacClough, I wasn't taking any chances. And in spite of Barnum's printed silence, I guess part of me could still hear her chanting Johnny's name.

I was busy renewing my amazement with truly white snow when my tiresome phone chirped me out of my trance.

"Yeah." I could be such a charmer.

"Detective Sergeant Mickelson, Suffolk County Police. Is Mr. Klein at home?"

"Speaking," I wondered if the bored detective could hear my intestines twisting into knots. "What can I do for you?"

"We have your sweater back from the lab," Mickelson yawned into his mouthpiece. "The tests came out negative, like we figured."

"Good thing," I laughed nervously. "My travel agent was havin' a tough time bookin' me a first-class room in Rio."

He greeted my weak levity with a long dose of silence. Then: "You can pick the garment up at this address during normal business hours."

"Thank you, detective. I'll probably be down today," I offered too cheerfully.

"Ain't that grand. Maybe we should put the Christmas lights back up," Mickelson chided. "Oh, by the way, Mr. Klein, since you're coming in, why don't ya stop by my office for a few minutes. See ya, let's say, within the hour."

The click and dial tone told me I would have to save my witty repartee until we spoke in person. I threw on my collection of silver zippers, suede laces and black leather that the world called a motorcycle jacket. I didn't have the pierced ear and Harley to complete the image. Christ, I didn't even own a Schwinn.

It wasn't much of an office, really. More like an appliance box with the top missing. Mickelson wasn't at his desk. I imagine that was intentional. He was giving me time to sweat and my pores were putting the minutes to good use. Sweat was good. Nerves were good. Years ago, MacClough had schooled me on that:

"Most people can't help actin' nervous and guilty

around cops. Even fuckin' priests and house pets get the jitters in the presence of guns and badges. Cops are used to people being uncomfortable around 'em. The perps are the cool ones. They've usually been through it all before. The cool ones; those are the ones we didn't trust. Not that we trusted anybody."

When Mickelson came in I was wiping my palms off on my own black jeans.

"You giving the bunt sign or starting a fire?" the thick necked detective asked rhetorically.

He pressed down on my shoulder with a big meaty paw when I tried standing to meet him. I recognized his face as one of those I'd told my story to on the night of the railroad execution. The face had registered, but so had a lot of others.

"Here," he reached into a drawer, pulled out Johnny's old bar sweater and tossed it to me.

The weathered wool wasn't any worse for wear, not that it could get much worse. I folded the old soldier up and tucked it under my arm. The detective just sort of sat there, saying nothing, watching me.

"Will that be all?" I asked after reaching my discomfort threshold.

"Mostly, yeah," Mickelson grunted. "You can go."

"Then why did you drag—" my voice was in mid-crescendo when he cut me off.

"Don't get indignant, Mr. Klein," he waved me and my voice back down. "I guess I wanted to let you know we're not as stupid as you might think. Do you really imagine that we swallowed that line of shit you fed us on the night of the murder? Come on. We're human. We wanted to go home for the holiday. But now all the gifts are open and the turkey's all finished."

"What's this all about, Mickelson," I challenged.

"You tell me, Klein. Your story had some gaps in it. Details were missing. That's pretty clear. We just can't figure out why, exactly. My gut tells me you're protecting someone. And my gut," he rubbed his Buddha belly, "is seldom wrong."

His belly wasn't wrong, but something else most definitely was. If MacClough had been in and talked it all out, why was I here? That night at the Rusty Scupper, MacClough had clearly stated that everything was taken care of. Maybe I hadn't listened closely enough or maybe I was just drunk. There was a third possibility. Maybe Johnny was lying.

"Detective Mickelson, did you ever talk to John Mac-Clough?" I questioned straight out.

"The ex-cop bar owner?" he yawned back. "Sure. Don't fret, Klein, he vouched for you. Seemed like a good guy, for a city cop."

"That's all he did?" I blurted out, regretting the question as soon as it left my lips.

"What did you want him to do?" The heavyset detective leaned forward with sudden interest.

"Nothin'," I feigned indifference and stood to go.

"So long, Mr. Klein. I just wanted to let you know that I'll figure it out. And when I get to the bottom of it, I hope you're not there. Why don't you tell me who you're covering for and be done with it?"

I ignored that and asked a question of my own. "Any word on who the dead woman was?"

"Why?" His face showed little real interest, but his raised eyebrows said different.

"I don't know. Curious, I guess. I was the last one to see her alive." That was amongst the ten stupidest things I've ever said and I've said a lot of stupid things.

"Not unless you killed her you weren't. Now get out of here before I put you back on the suspect list." Mickelson pointed to the door and began punching up a phone number.

"Well . . ." I waited.

"You still here?" he looked properly annoyed. "What? What?"

"About the dead woman."

"She died a Jane Doe. She's still a Jane Doe. And my gut tells me . . ."

I was out of the appliance box before he could finish the sentence. I'd heard enough about his belly for one day. The witch's curse was back and haunting me again. In the car I ran through a list of excuses and maybes that might account for the discrepancy between Mickelson's telling and MacClough's.

"That's it!" I slapped the wheel and screamed to no one but me. Johnny had spoken to another detective Mickelson was probably in charge of one part of the investigation and there was another detective, maybe ten other detectives, handling different aspects of the case. Lord knows, there were enough cops at the Scupper that night to divide the case a hundred ways and still have leftovers.

The Scupper was chilly and empty of paying customers. MacClough stood behind the bar sipping a long Bushmills, staring glassy-eyed through the front window across Main Street at Stan Long's desolate self-service pumps. Patsy Cline's "Crazy" was just finishing its twirl on the Wurlitzer. That was odd. Johnny hated that song. He'd reset the jukebox every time it came on and claim the record was too scratchy. Maybe his last patron had played it. No matter.

The red golf sweater I'd gifted him for Christmas was busy being broken in. I liked him better in the old one. I'd left the old one in my car. Johnny couldn't know I had it yet. That would be tipping my hand.

Just as I hitched my heel onto the bar rail, "Crazy" came on again.

"Hey!" I snapped my fingers at MacClough.

There was moisture—tears, I thought—in Johnny's eyes

as he turned in my direction. But before the salt water could roll out onto his ruddy cheeks, the barman rubbed them away.

"Goddamn air's too dry in here. Irritates my eyes," he offered nonchalantly and rubbed some more. "I'll get a humidifier and fix that right up."

"Yeah and while you're fixin' things around here, you can have someone look at the jukebox," I threw my head that way.

"Huh?" he squinted, not understanding. "Oh!" the ex-cop hit the reset button. "You know, I wasn't even listening. I hate that song. What brings you here?" Mac-Clough wanted to know, sounding almost normal.

"Well, it's been a while since the murder and I haven't heard from the cops," I lied.

"And you shouldn't."

"But what if they call? What was the name of the cop you spoke to?" I swallowed my words, but he heard the questions.

"Why?"

"This way if another detective hassles me, I can refer him to the detective you spoke to," I answered, plausibly I thought. "Maybe it'll save me a trip to the station."

"Mickelson," Johnny took a sip of his Irish. "A short, fat guy named Mickelson."

I felt sick, heartsick. There was a lump in my throat bigger than a breadbox, but smaller than Rhode Island. Only a litttle smaller, though. MacClough was lying to me. I was fresh out of fancy explanations. Kate Barnum was right. Johnny was involved in the Christmas murder, maybe even a second. Why else would he be giving me the business?

He couldn't have forgotten I was wearing his sweater when I found the woman's body. He'd know there was a fair chance they'd return the sweater to me when the tests were complete. Could it be MacClough was just being sloppy? The John MacClough I knew was never sloppy, especially about police work and procedure. But then again, the John MacClough I knew wasn't a murderer nor much of a liar. Maybe I didn't know John MacClough at all. I was determined to find out.

"Hey!" this time the barman was snapping at *me*. "Here," Johnny put a coaster and a brown frothy brew down at my station.

"No thanks," I waved it off and stood to go. "Not feeling well."

"Maybe it's the weather."

"Yeah," I conceded, "or maybe it's just the air in here." I was gone.

Blue Moons

Start with what you have. That's what MacClough had always counseled. But what did I have? A lot of smoke and innuendo, at least one lie and an orphaned heart. I didn't really even have that anymore. Who did? Johnny did. That was my bet. I could draw the heart, its little gold hands and diamonds. I could draw it and I did.

Cassius had nothing on Larry Feld when it came to lean and hungry. He'd always been gaunt, even as a six-year-old. The hunger came with age. Larry's eternally meager flesh was covered in black crocodile loafers, matching belt and a steel gray, woolen suit with angle-cuffed trousers. His neck was so thin that the starchy white collar of his shirt and the shantung paisley tie that slid through it hung a thumb's width off his apparent Adam's apple.

Larry Feld was just another kid from the old block, a childhood friend by default. His parents were fat, somber people with forearm tattoos they hadn't gotten as a lark on an all-night drunk. No, they'd seen more than just dreams go up in smoke. The blue moons they'd seen were the by-products of burning relatives distorting the night's reflected sunlight. And they'd raised their son to bear their crosses well.

As is too often the case, the children of victims transform themselves into victimizers. Larry epitomized the process. He always took unnatural joy in getting over, in cheating. When we were kids, Larry's specialty was convincing a cashier he'd paid her with a twenty when it'd only been a ten spot. It was Larry Feld against the world. Not just every now and then, but for every breath.

None of this is to say Larry wasn't a hard worker. On the contrary, he took jobs none of the other guys would have even considered. All Larry asked of a job was that it afford him the opportunity to fuck the public where they breathed. As long as it provided that certain slant, it was meat for Mr. Feld. He pumped gas—mid-winter, graveyard shift—during the first oil crisis. With almost sexual ecstasy, Larry would recount tales of extortion. How he'd garnered huge sums of cash from drivers desperate for a few extra gallons of unleaded. Our moral outrage was tempered, however, by Larry's ability to get our families a tankful on demand at pre-extortion prices.

With two oil shortages behind him, Larry bankrolled himself through three years at Brooklyn Law. Eventually, he squeaked by the New York Bar and his practice took off like a missile to Mars. Lawrence Solomon Feld did certainly shine in the world or torts and tarts and litigation. Positioning himself to profit from human misfortune and disaster was Larry's particular niche in the food chain. Not all vultures have feathers.

I hated going to Larry. It was Larry who supplied me with a career and direction when I had neither. He'd gotten me into the investigations racket. He schooled me in the basics of the work. And after I was done teething on some easy jobs that paid too much, he set me up in an office. Neither one of us labored under any false notions about his charity or my drive and ability. Trust was the issue. Larry trusted me more than he trusted most. It was a vestigal bond left over from childhood.

I don't think I liked Larry more than the other kids on the block. I'm not certain liking him was even an option. You sort of tolerated Larry and in return he rewarded you with the profits of his misdeeds. I guess I was less two-faced in my toleration. The other guys would ask Larry along, but give him the wrong meeting time or place. I wouldn't hold for that. I would either correct the misinformation or just hang with Larry. Sometimes I laughed at my naive nobility. At other times, I wondered where it had gone.

Our business relationship worked pretty smoothly for a while. He fed me plenty of jobs and he knew he could take my reports at face value; nothing faked, nothing fabricated. When he didn't have cases for me, he'd refer other lawyers my way. I was making a living. And if I wasn't Philip Marlowe, I was, at least, competent.

Things got rough when Larry's bill came due and I refused to pay. His clientele was changing. Cases involving old Haitian women with whiplash were being given to the firm's fledglings or farmed out to other shops altogether. I started recognizing the names on case files as those I'd read in the newspapers. In a two-year span Larry defended a list of accused that might have made Beelzebub blush.

There was the yuppie doctor who was charged with first-degree sexual assault and second-degree murder for strangling his kid's babysitter with a stethoscope. I helped find another of the dead girl's clients who'd slept with her. Larry twisted the rape and murder into accidental death during voluntary sexual relations. The stethoscope, you see, was being used to heighten the babysitter's orgasm. The doctor spent less time in Attica than he had at Johns Hopkins.

There were other cases, all notorious. Hey, I wasn't thrilled, but I've always been an ace at rationalization. No, the problems came when Larry started handling organized crime cases. That's when the tab came due. At first he added small tasks to my caseload. I had to drop this off or pick that up or . . . You know, little things, little favors. I was becoming a better bagman than investigator. Bagman paid better.

One day my job description took too big a leap. A leap I wouldn't take no matter how good the pay. One of

Larry's big Mafia trials wasn't going at all well and he figured a mistrial was better than the certain guilty verdict. He met me in a diner in the Bronx and passed two attaché cases full of hundreds underneath the table to me. I was supposed to plant the money in one juror's car and bury the second case in another's backyard. I left the diner and Larry and the bag money behind. I owed Larry, but not that much.

I hated going back to him. But it's in the nature of people like Larry to be acquainted with almost everyone, to have feelers everywhere. For one thing, he knew the Diamond Exchange inside and out. His somber little parents had run a booth there since after the war. That would help with the orphaned heart. He'd also have connections in the Police Department. His word could get me in doors I couldn't even knock on. I needed him and that was a bad spot to be in, a very bad spot indeed.

"Dylan," his voice and handshake were welcoming and firm. "You like?" He caught my eyes staring over his shoulder at a still photo of Mike Wallace, himself and his latest Mafia client, Dante "Don Juan" Gandolfo, during an interview on *60 Minutes*.

"Nice shot," I flattered. "I see your taste in clients hasn't changed," I added foolishly.

"Klein. Klein. Klein," Larry shook his oval, high crowned head. "What am I gonna do with you? What's it five, six years—"

"Seven," I corrected, "but who's counting?"

"I haven't seen or spoken to you in seven years and you're already busting my chops. But that's you, Klein, isn't it? You should have been one of King Arthur's knights, a hero, someone to read about, someone from a time of honor. Tell me, Sir Knight, did such a time ever exist?"

"Sorry, Larry. I was outta line." And I was.

"So," he poured his lank into a black leather and tubular

steel chair behind his desk and waved me into a similar
model on my side, "what is it?"

"What is it?" I repeated dumbly.

"You need something. You want something. Something
needs fixing. What? What? What?" Larry shot off rapid
fire, his Adam's apple skittering up and down his neck
like a mouse caught in a garden hose.

"Here," I handed him my rendition of the diamond
heart.

"I've got a lot of pull in this town," my ex-employer
commented, still surveying my drawing, "but even I
couldn't get you into art school."

"That's not—" I started to explain.

"I know what you want, Sir Knight. What's it made
out of?"

"White gold and diamonds."

"You want to know who handles this kinda piece at the
exchange?" Larry smiled with that old chilling look of
self-satisfaction.

"Who?" I found myself standing, hands on his desk.

"Can't tell ya." He looked disapprovingly at my hands
until I withdrew them and sat back down. "But I know
who can."

"Who?" I asked again without unseating myself.

"Mojo," was his reply.

"Mojo? Mojo who?"

"Don't worry about Mojo who. Use my name and any-
one who knows his *tush* from his tits will put you onto
Mojo. Here," he flipped one of his business cards at me.
"Is that it?"

"One thing more." I put forth weakly.

"That is . . ."

"Got an ex-detective for a friend these days. I wanna
throw him a big bash, but I don't know how to get in
touch with his old buddies and partners. I figured you
could get me a list without alerting anyone's attention."

"Name?"

"John Francis MacClough. Rhymes with cow," I added out of habit.

"You'll have your list tomorrow. I won't be in, but I'll leave it at the front desk."

"Thank's, Larry," I was up, extending my hand for a good-bye shake.

Cassius wasn't having any of it. I wouldn't be exiting just yet. His cold gaze directed me back to my seat.

"Mary," he pressed a button and spoke into a speaker box, "come in a minute. You," Larry turned to me, "want anything?"

I shook him off. The longest ten seconds I'd ever experienced went by before Mary, a stern-faced woman of the middle years and the bulging middle, trotted her rasping pantyhose over to Larry's desk.

"Call Billy Minter at One Police Plaza. Get me a copy of this guy's file," Mary plucked the paper with Johnny's name on it out of her boss's fingers. "I want to know who his partners were, the whole nine yards. And if Minter, that fat fuck, gives you a hard time, put him on the line."

Mary was gone.

"I hear you're an author these days," Larry focused back on me.

"I write."

"I've read all of it. It's good."

I nodded my thanks and surprise.

"Yeah, I read it. That's why I thought you came here today. I thought maybe you needed a little help in getting an agent or a contract. But no." Larry did a rare thing. He laughed, really. "That's not you, Klein," the laughing came to an abrupt end. "You wouldn't come to me for yourself. Not you. Not Sir Knight."

"Look Larry—"

"Don't 'look Larry' me. Don't you dare. I appreciated what you did for me as a kid, Klein. That's why there was no fallout last time. I closed that account a long time ago," Larry wiped his bony hands past one another twice. "I'm a powerful man now and my favors cost considerably more than my legal services. These days I pull more strings than Harpo Marx. Do we understand one another?"

I indicated that I did.

"Good," Larry twisted his thin lips into an approximation of a smile. "This time, Sir Dylan, when I ask for a favor in return, don't disappoint me."

We didn't shake hands. You didn't need to shake with the devil. I had my hand on the door when the fallen angel called out to me.

"Party! Big bash, huh. Don't forget to invite me. I'm a lot of things, Klein, but stupid isn't one of 'em. I just hope this cop's worth it to you."

So did I.

Mr. Fancy Picasso

"Mojo?" the hefty, black security guard smiled, resting his hand carelessly on the handle of his Magnum. "You'll find Mojo down the second isle on your right, third stall on your right. Can't miss Mojo."

But apparently I had. I stood in front of a small grubby booth. The cheaply engraved plaque read, "Minkowitz, Inc.-Purveyors of Fine Gems and Jewels." Seated on a shaky piano stool behind the low wall and glass was a sour-looking Hasidic man in his late forties, early fifties maybe. The wiry salt and pepper beard and curls made a more accurate guess impossible. He wore a dandruff-speckled yarmulke held in place with a worn shiny hairpin. Currently he was inspecting a herd of small diamonds laid out on his sickly pale and pudgy palm.

I watched him. His concentration was incredible, and he manipulated the little stones with an ease and confidence that seemed more instinctive than learned. Occasionally he would remove his black-rimmed glasses, the joints of which were held together with bandaids, shove an eyepiece into his left eye and hold the clear rocks up to his face. All very interesting, but I had to find Mojo. I started back to the security guard.

"I'm who you're lookin' for mister," the man behind the Minkowitz sign called to me without picking his head up from the stones. His voice had that familiar roller coaster lilt of a Yiddish speaker.

"Sorry," I came back over, "not buying today."

"From me, you couldn't afford to buy," he let the dia-

monds roll off his palms like so much dust into a folded
paper envelope. "You lookin' for Mojo? I'm Mojo."

"Mojo Monkowitz?" everything about me was in-
credulous.

"Listen *totaleh,* vit a last name like Minkowitz, vould it
matta vhat vent in front?" he asked in an accent thick like
chicken fat on rye bread.

"You got a point. How—"

"Before we start with the questions, he cut me off, returning to a less theatrical dialect, "who sent you? Nobody
comes to Mojo without being sent."

I handed him Larry's business card and my infantile
drawing of the heart. He read the card, looked at the drawing and shook his head.

"You friends with this man?" Mojo inquired, holding
up the business card.

"We grew up together. Did a little work together. I
wouldn't call us friends."

"Good. Larry Feld is not a righteous man," Minkowitz
sat down and inspected my artwork. "I knew his parents.
Good people. Sad little people, but they ran a clean shop.
You knew them, Izzi and Anna?"

"Lived two doors down from 'em for eighteen years.
But it's hard to really know camp survivors," I offered
my opinion.

"Quite so," he showed me his numerical tattoo. "I do
these favors not for the son, but for the pain of the parents.
You understand this?" He seemed anxious that I understand
and I nodded that I did. "You want to know who handles
pieces like this, who makes pieces like this?"

"That's the big question."

"Describe a little better what the piece is made out of.
How many stones? How big?"

I gave him the specs to the best of my memory. As I
did, he shook his head in agreement as if I was simply
reinforcing the conclusion he'd already arrived at.

"Fischel Kahn," Mojo winked. "Fine work. Not much
demand for his stuff anymore."

"Where's his booth?"

"Four aisles over, but he's retired maybe fifteen twenty years already. Sold his business to an Iraqi Jew," Mojo's sour expression returned. Despite the monolithic image, there were large groups of Jews that couldn't stomach one another.

"Shi—" I stopped myself. "Sorry."

"Quiet. Quiet," Minkowitz waved off my apology and began stroking his beard as if it were a Siamese cat. "Can't a man think a little?" A moment passed. "Sylvia . . . Sylvia . . . Sylvia Kim!" Mojo's eyes lit up.

"Kim? An Asian?" I wondered.

"Used to be Kimmelmann. Now it's Kim. She's got her own shop. Next aisle over. Once worked for Fish. Maybe she can help," he handed me Larry's card and my rendering and shook my hand. "*Mazel* and *brucha,* luck and a blessing to you on your journey."

"I understood. Thanks. What do I owe you?"

"Like I said before," the survivor admonished, "from me you can't afford to buy."

"You think she'll remember the piece?" I questioned as an afterthought, pointing at my drawing.

"Listen, Mr. Fancy Picasso with the drawing already. If she was around when the piece was sold, she'll remember. We're very good at remembering." He looked at his tattoo and went back to work.

Sylvia had frosty blond hair that was blown and permed and sprayed into submission. Her teeth were as white as the Himalayas and as natural as astroturf. The skin on her face was Florida tanned and taut as if it were a plastic bag stretched to its limit. Her flaming nails weren't quite as long as piano keys and there was so much jewelry on her fingers, I could barely see the flesh. She was covered in enough metal and mineral to cover half the Periodic Chart. I wondered if she floated when the hardware came off.

But none of it affected her memory.

"Nice couple. Nice couple." She got a far away look in her violet contact lenses. "He was a roughly handsome boy, German, Irish maybe. She was a looker, a Jewish girl. She spoke the language." I took that to mean Yiddish. "Had a figure to die for and the features of a goddess. They were a funny pair."

I described Johnny and Jane Doe to Sylvia.

"Could be them. Got a picture?" she asked.

"Sorry."

"Got a girlfriend? she winked at me with black lashes as long as butterfly wings.

"Sure do," I lied.

"Now I'm the one who's sorry. What's this all about?" Rejected, she suddenly got curious.

I showed her Larry's card.

"Why didn't you say so?" We were friends again. "Anything else I can do for you? Anything at all?"

"No thanks, Sylvia. Here," I gave her one of my old business cards with the office number scratched out and my home number scribbled in. "If there's something else that you recall about the couple or the piece, even if it seems trivial or insignificant, call me."

"Maybe," she read my card, "Dylan Klein, I'll just call you." If nothing else, Sylvia was persistent.

I kissed the back of her right hand, nearly slicing a lip open in the process, took one of her cards and was gone. On the way out onto West 47th Street, I bumped into the security guard I'd met on the way in.

"Did you find Mojo, all right?" he laughed and slapped my shoulder playfully. "Don't look much like a Mojo, does he?"

"No, I had to admit that. "How did—"

"—he get that nickname?" the jolly guard finished my question. "Some big gambler give it to him. Said he had to get his Mojo workin' and bought a big piece from Mr. Minkowitz. Gambler went to Vegas and practically shut down three casinos. Gamblers been comin' ever since. You know, to get their Mojo workin'. Moshe. Mojo. It just kinda stuck."

"Not a very kosher name for a Hasidic Jew," I mused.

"I wouldn't know about that. Excuse me," the guard turned his attention to a group of five kids coming through the door. "Can I help you?"

An inch of gray snow came between my feet and the concrete on 6th Avenue. More of it fell onto my nearly defenseless scalp, melting quickly and cascading down my neck as a dirty stream of water. Running-shoed women with newspaper umbrellas elbowed themselves into other people's taxis. Buses threw slushy gutter puddles up onto tailored pant legs and nyloned ankles. No one took much notice. They could take it. They were New Yorkers. They could take anything. The problem was, they often did.

The Cursing Millions

Time wasn't quite standing still.

I was laughing, listening to the radio telling me how bad the traffic was. Oh, New Yorkers could deal with almost any adversity, but driving in a steady snow wasn't one of them. Four inches of packed powder could bring mighty Gotham to its knees. Just ask the driver in front of me or the one in front of her or the driver behind me or the one behind him. Maybe you should just take my word for it. By now, no one in a car in Manhattan was in any mood to answer questions.

I was laughing because this oil and water mixture of New Yorkers and snow is what had helped to kill a nuclear power plant on Long Island. In order to fire up a nuclear reactor you need to have an evacuation plan. Unfortunately, since Long Island is an island, the only viable means of mass evacuation is over the road through New York City. Even on a holiday in perfect weather, driving to and from New York is a nightmare worthy of a movie. As you might anticipate, it was rather an arduous task for the utility to put a positive spin on an over-the-road evacuation thru the city. But never underestimate the stupidity of bureaucrats. Never!

They were about to pass the plan. I guess the geniuses in Washington thought New York City residents were so tough, they wouldn't try to save themselves. No, they'd just clear the roads and let their Long Island brethren pass right on through. Oh sure they would. And when they were done waving good-bye to the Long Islanders, the

New Yorkers would all climb onto their rooftops, face due east toward the impending meltdown and collectively shout: "Fuck you, radiation. We can take it."

Just when this ridiculous scheme was ready to sail, some stick-in-the-mud, liberal, left-wing radical, environmentally active, pinko, oddball kook asked this question: What if it snows? Troublemakers! God, don't ya just hate 'em? Well, eventually the state bought the plant and shut it down. So I guess we'll never know what will happen if it snows.

My sputtering Volkswagen was about twenty feet closer to the Queens Midtown Tunnel than it had been just forty minutes ago. The hands on my watch moved even more slowly. But like I said, time wasn't quite standing still. I had an eternity of seconds to laugh and ponder there in the snow and fumes and hardening dark slush. I shut my eyes and saw the cursing millions on their rooftops. I saw angry black children leaping from car roof to car roof trying to fly. I saw the jaws of the earth open, swallowing all the foolish men. I saw myself getting home sometime in early April. I opened my eyes and found the nearest hotel.

The Hindenburg

The Hotel St. Lawrence was a nondescript soot-faced building buried somewhere on Lexington Avenue below 34th Street. Its heritage could not be described as proud nor even once-proud. It'd never been a poets' or musicians' haunt like The Chelsea. Jack Kennedy and Marilyn Monroe hadn't slept there, so The Waldorf was safe. And at last check, the rat pack, brat pack, jet set and royalty still preferred The Plaza, Pierre and St. Moritz. What the Hotel St. Lawrence offered was rooms, plenty of them and, unlike the aforementioned establishments, at prices a little less inflated than the Hindenburg.

Actually, business at the front desk was pretty brisk, but not brisk enough for management to break out the "No Vacancy" sign. I had my pick of rooms. Wow! I could face brick, steel, or the street. I picked a room with the view, surrendered my credit card and got my key. How novel; a hotel that still used keys. It was real metal and everything, not some encoded piece of plastic. I hurried through the slip cover and green velveteen lobby and into the Seaway Lounge.

Just outside the cocktail quarters, an entire wall was covered in black and white publicity photos of mostly dead and totally forgotten comics. I went in anyway. I'd been in worse bars. I'd sat on less comfortable stools. I'd gotten slower, ruder service from nastier barmen and sipped flatter beer from dirtier glasses. I'd even seen uglier wallpaper in an acid flashback once. But, having noted all this, I wouldn't bet that I'd be back at the Seaway Lounge anytime soon.

The room was an improvement. Not a quantum leap, mind you, but a step up. Its last facelift had been done when younger men wore acetate shirts and platform shoes. There were starving artist prints on the walls, but mercifully, no dead comics. The TV reception looked more like a blizzard than my view onto Lexington Avenue. Maybe I'd be headed back to the bar sooner than expected.

I dialed Kate Barnum's number at *The Whaler*. I was ready to deal. Being indebted to Larry Feld made bargaining with Barnum seem like a minor detail. She wasn't in. I tried her shack in Dugan's Dump and listened to the phone ring endlessly. I stopped listening and lay back on the bed.

Somebody drummed their knuckles against the door. I let them drum for a bit before answering. And like some witless schmuck, I just flung the door open without inquiry.

"Queen-sized bed," Kate Barnum commented, looking beyond my shoulder. "That's good." She sounded as if she'd made a short detour at the Seaway Lounge before coming my way. "Take this," the reporter shoved a brown paper bag into my hands and removed her coat. The bag contained some bags of bar nuts, barbecue chips, a full bottle of Grand Marnier and a six pack of Diet Coke.

"You've been—" I began.

She cut me off with a light kiss. "Yes, Klein, I've been following you around all day. You're quite the fellow about town. That's a fascinating assortment of acquaintances you've got, but we can talk about that later. I am tired of talking just now."

She kissed me again and I returned the favor in the growing darkness. The flavors on her tongue—orange, smoke and brandy—began to overwhelm my senses. The kisses deepened quickly without the pretense of challenge and surrender. There seemed an urgent sadness in all of this, a hemorrhaging emptiness and not all of it hers. But as I pulled her familiar sweater off, the apparent urgency diminished.

"Wait," Burnum demanded, literally holding me at arms length. She reached into the goody bag which I'd unconsciously let fall at the first sign of passion. The bottle of Grand Marnier appeared in her hand. She broke the seal and took a prodigious gulp. She put the bottle down and finished undressing without my help. I walked to the bed. That seemed to please her. But when I reached for my belt buckle, she shook her head violently. That would be her job, her candy.

I rolled over. She was at the bottle again. She turned the bottle over on her bare breasts and rubbed the resulting stream into the thin patch of hair below her waist. Barnum turned to me, seemingly startled that I was watching. I took the bottle, then a drink, and then her.

Her breasts were surprisingly solid, sticky to the touch and sweet to my taste. Her nipples spread wide over the front of her breasts and their bloom was brownish. I had dreamed them differently, but their real feel and flavor did not disappoint. I played hard with the bumpy brown circles of skin, capturing her erect nipple between my top and bottom teeth.

"Bite, goddamit. Bite!" a breathless voice begged.

I bit hard, very hard.

"Christ!" she cried. I'm . . . I'm . . " her body arched like the back of a bronco, throwing me off to the side.

I moved to mount her, but she held back.

"Wait," she coughed in the deepening night and fumbled along the rug. "Here," she handed me what might've been a wet nap, but since we weren't eating ribs or lobster . . .

I didn't put it on and tried to move my mouth along the dried brandy river, into her positively soaked crotch.

"No!" she pushed me off the bed, her feet against my shoulders.

When I crawled back up, I found her knees down, tucked and spread. Her head faced away from me and a pillow was wedged under her breasts. The full pink of her lips seemed to glisten with a light of their own. I rolled the latex on and went looking for that light.

As I was about to enter she reached back and guided my penis into a spot above where I was aiming. God, it was tight and I could feel the muscles fairly close around me. A groan rose up from Kate Barnum that spoke volumes of the thin lines separating pleasure and pain.

"God, Dylan," she gasped. "Hard. Just hard."

I pounded into her, slapping my mass against her with each thrust. It was over quickly for me. The explosion burned right through me, so intensely that I couldn't judge whether any of this was hard enough or long enough to suit Kate Barnum.

I staggered into the bathroom. She followed. We showered in silence. We didn't kiss. We touched only through the medium of soap. None of it had been about romance anyway. Punishment? Manipulation? Maybe. But surely not romance . . . Our fucking was food shared between the starving, food we might otherwise have ignored.

"I need you to find out what you can about the dead woman," I spoke straight out. We were back in bed, ignoring what had just passed between us.

"Why? Can't his royal highness, Larry Feld, defender of any and all scumbugs be bothered with such small details?" she asked with feigned surprise.

"Next question," I waved her on.

"What was the trip to the Diamond Ex—"

"Let's get something straight," I stepped on her words. "You're gonna get your fucking story. I was ringing your house when you knocked. But how I dig and why I dig is my turf. Don't step on it. When I ask *you* to dig," I flattened her nose with my left index finger. "You dig. I'll worry about what your shovel brings up," I pulled my finger in. "I want to know about the dead woman."

"Yes Tarzan," Barnum mocked me with a bow, her still bare breasts brushing the covers. "But if I can't come along for the ride, what guarantees do I have that you're giving it to me straight?"

"My word."

"Your word?" She lit a cigarette.

"That's all you get," I grabbed the cigarette and took a puff. "And if," I coughed the smoke out with my threat, "I catch you pullin' what you pulled today, it's no deal. No story. Don't follow me again. Don't have me followed. I'll be lookin' now."

"I get the whole story, unedited, unwashed?"

"Dirty as a clamdigger's toenails," I assured her.

"Let's drink on it. Pass me the Grand Marnier," she pointed out its hiding place.

I leaned over the bed's edge, recouped the quarter-filled bottle and took a choking swig. Kate Barnum snatched the bottle, matched my swallow and killed the bedside lamp. She moved near me and let the remainder of the bottle flow into my lap. Even in the blackness, I could see that she had moved to clean up the latest puddle. She cleaned and I let her.

Someone Else's Toy

Kate Barnum had gone. The sun was strong. Most of the snow had turned itself into sewer juice. And the list of John Francis MacClough's former partners was waiting for me at Larry Feld's office. I tried to strike up a conversation with his secretary, but she blew me off like last year's lint. She did, however, give me a condescending scowl when she noticed that my attire hadn't changed since yesterday. I didn't take it too much to heart and left Mary to wither and die. Hopefuly, sooner than later.

The top four or five names were familiar to me. I'd already met some of these guys at Emerald Society functions MacClough had dragged me to. One or two of them had even graced the Rusty Scupper with their presence. They'd be easy enough to talk to. Lord knows, they seemed to have an endless stream of Johnny MacClough stories.

It was John's early running mates that concerned me. They were old school boys from a time when patrolling a beat meant using your feet and not a steering wheel. In their day, all lunches were free, drinks were always on the house and everyone in the precinct had pockets padded by local businessmen. Their weakness for the pay-off wasn't at issue. It was accepted by everyone, except Al Pacino, and condoned at the highest levels. It's just that old-timers didn't believe in talking to non-cops. That was a real barrier. That and the fact that one of John's ex-compatriots was five years with the angels and another lived in Yuma, Arizona.

Cops, all cops, are such suspicious bastards. I'd have to tread lightly, but not so lightly as to reap no results. It would be like tap dancing around a land mine. One misstep, one wrong question and they'd tip Johnny to my game. I couldn't afford to have things blow up in my face; not yet, anyway. I decided to use the wheeze about throwing Johnny a big party and how it was a total surprise type deal and, while we're on the subject, do you remember any of his old flames? The line hadn't worked on Larry Feld, but nothing ever fooled Larry and I was fresh out of alternative ploys.

I started by calling on the cops I'd met and moved onto the ones I'd heard Johnny mention in stories or in passing. Some of them were still on the job. Some were in various states of retirement. By nightfall I'd been in every borough of the city, seen the insides of three precinct houses, walked the floor at Bloomingdale's with the assistant head of security and shared overcooked shepherd's pie with one of John's ex-partners who ran a failing Irish pub in Greenpoint. By nightfall I'd run out of even vaguely familiar names. By nightfall I'd been almost everywhere, but gotten nowhere.

Oh, my approach seemed to go over smoothly enough. I got a warehouse full of feedback on the subject of John Francis MacClough, but nothing in the warehouse was worth my while. Everyone wanted in on the party for Johnny. Everyone offered to help. Everyone loved MacClough. Everyone had a few choice Johnny MacClough stories. Everyone told me his favorite. Everyone remembered the sergeant's wife Johnny had porked on a dare or the Puerto Rican deli girl who went down on Johnny in a beer cooler during the '77 Blackout or Johnny and the twin nurses. No one remembered anyone who fit the dead woman's description. No one recalled Johnny ever having a pet name or a nickname. Certainly not Johnny Blue.

I made two more stops on my trek back to Sound Hill. One for gas and a piss in Syosset. The other detour had to do with a stranger's name on a list in my pocket.

Terrence O'Toole was an aging, pot-bellied giant with a red veiny nose to shame Rudolph and a manner crustier than week-old French bread. He answered his front door armed with a dangling cigarette, a can of Coors and an expression as sour as a barrel full of pickles.

"I don't know you," he accused, blowing smoke and the sick smell of burped up beer down to me.

"That's right. You don't."

"What you selling then? Nevermind," the giant raised a meaty paw to cut off any answer I might have. "Whatever it is, I don't want any. I don't need any." He stepped back and started closing the door.

"Wait a fuckin' second, goddamit!" I blurted out in unthinking frustration.

The door reversed its direction. A beer can fell and one of those huge hands snapped out at me like a lizard's tongue. Clamped firmly around my throat, it reeled me into the vestibule. O'Toole was one strong old man. He could easily have kicked my ass up and down the block without breaking a sweat.

"What was that, mister?" he tightened his grip about my neck. My head felt like an overfull water-balloon.

"John Mac—" I coughed, not having enough air for the last syllable.

"Who?" O'Toole loosened the lizard's tongue a bit.

"Johnny MacClough. I'm here about Johnny MacClough."

There was no further change in the relationship between his hand and my throat, but his sour face mellowed some and his eyes rolled back into his skull. I figured he was running over what was left of his memory. How much remained was a toss-up. Age takes it toll and noses don't get that red and veiny from the sun.

"What about Johnny?" the old cop had finished cross-referencing.

I didn't respond immediately, instead pointing to the proximity of his fingers and my windpipe. He made like Pharaoh and let me go. I was still a little nauseous and light headed, so O'Toole guided me—pushed me, really—into his kitchen and sat me down at the table. Something hissed like a rush of steam and an open can of beer appeared before me.

"Drink!" he ordered.

I drank.

"Now what's this about Johnny?"

I told him about the party.

"You're full of shit, mister," the old cop smiled at me for the first time with evil, crooked teeth. "You could just have easily called me about this party as shown up at my door at night in the middle of winter. Come on now, you can do better than that. You couldn't fool my dead granny with that party yarn. What gives?"

"Nothin'," I stood up to go. "Forget it. Sorry I bothered you."

"No ya don't," something quick and powerful shoved me back into my seat.

"I didn't make detective, but don't ever mistake that for stupidity. I just never looked good in a suit. Now spill."

I spilled. I spilled like an open milk carton turned upside down. He heard it all. He heard all about my Christmas Eve. He heard all about the ratty mink coat, Johnny Blue, my broken pint glass and the orphaned heart.

He saw tracks in the snow and blood in the snow and death in the snow. I introduced him to Kate, Larry, Mojo, Sylvia and the pinky-ringed sapling in Dugan's Dump. He listened without emotion, taking it in with a sip now and then. He burped like a cannon when I finished.

"She had some funny kinda name," the giant finger-combed his thin wisps of white hair. "Something biblical. Andrella, maybe. Something like that. I don't know. Christ, it was a fucking lifetime ago."

"You remember the girl?" I jumped up.

"Are you deaf, boy?" he growled and pointed me back to my seat. " I had Johnny straight outta the academy; greener than clover and chestier than a motherfucker. But he had the curse of instinct. A natural born cop, that one. Could smell trouble a block before I could see it and I was no slouch."

I didn't doubt it.

"Johnny," the giant continued, reaching for a bottle of Murphy's Irish, "only had one blind spot."

"The girl," I offered.

"The girl," he accepted with a nod. "I tried warning him off her, but Johnny was a kid. Kids don't listen. See him," pickle face pointed to an ornately framed photo of an elephant-eared boy in Marine blues. "That was my son. Told him not to join up. Coulda gotten him onto the force, but kids don't listen. Got himself killed during Tet. It killed his mother too." The bitter man lobbed his shot glass at the photo and missed.

"What about the girl?" I tried to snap O'Toole out of his foggy reminiscence.

"Don't know that much about her," red-nose admitted, drinking directly from the bottle. "Johnny was smart enough not to discuss her around me once he figured I disapproved. That's—"

"Disapproved," I cut in. "Why?"

"She was someone else's toy. And from what I could sniff out, that someone else was family connected. Do you get my meaning?"

"Mafia."

"Bingo, boy. You win a drink. Here," he stuck the Murphy's in my fist.

I didn't want a drink, but I plugged the bottle with my tongue and made believe. The tip of my tongue didn't like it, but the rest of me appreciated the pantomime.

"The bitch was a Jew to boot," the giant grabbed the bottle back.

Maybe something showed on my face. I don't know, but O'Toole squinted at me.

"What's your name anyways?" He tried dressing the question up with an air of nonchalance, but his self-consciousness was showing.

"Klein. Dylan Klein," I replied with as little affect as possible.

He just smirked, threw up his free palm and raised his brows. That was as much of an apology as I was going to get. And I wasn't about to push him. I couldn't afford to plug the the only pumping well I'd struck so far. So what if he wasn't a flower child. Besides, hate was probably all he had left. I was so good at rationalization.

"So she was a wiseguy's girl and she didn't take communion." I put us back on track. "What else? What about Johnny Blue?"

"There ain't much else," he took a small ocean of a drink. "The Johnny Blue stuff was a code thing between 'em. Like I said, Johnny knew I disapproved. So she'd leave notes at the precinct house for Johnny Blue or Johnny Green. I didn't make detective," the booze was making him repeat things now, "but even I could figure that one color meant the coast was clear and the other was a warning."

"Anything else?" I pumped some more.

"See him?" O'Toole was pointing at his son's picture again. "Kids—

"—don't listen," I finished. "Johnny and the girl," I prodded.

"Right," he tried licking the bottom of the bottle. "Kids don't listen. Coulda gotten him onto the force."

I figured the well was running dry as the Murphy's and my time had come to leave. I planted one of my old business cards in his shirt pocket and reminded him to ignore the office number. I thanked him and asked him to call if anything, no matter how insignificant, about Johnny and the girl came to mind.

"Did I tell ya the cunt was a matzoh eater?" he smiled that evil-toothed smile up at me. His blue eyes were as glazed as a holiday ham. "Hey, get me a beer, fella, huh?"

"Yeah, you told me about the girl," I assured him, popping open a Coors. "Sleep tight," I handed him the beer knowing he would. I started for the front door.

"Crazy," the sour cop's voice boomed to my back.

I considered not turning to him, but I don't always pay atttention to what I'm thinking. "What?" I shouted.

"Crazy, I'm crazy for feelin' so lonely," the giant sang in a queer falsetto. "Johnny was always singin' that. I told ya." He hadn't. "The kid had some good pipes on him. I got him right outta the academy; greener than clover . . ."

I closed the door quietly behind me as the scarlet-nosed giant ate at his bitter heart and finished his drunken tape loop of stories.

Dark Pride

The only thing working hard the next morning was my dialing finger. O'Toole had finally given me some meat for my table. But when you spilled out all the fat and reduced it over high heat, there really wasn't much to chew on. I'd gotten just enough to eat to let let me know how hungry I really was.

I punched up Larry Feld's office. Much to my chagrin, his secretary was still alive. She didn't exactly treat my call like the second coming, but Mary managed to put me through before any more of my hair turned gray or fell out. I knew it was in my head, but the phone got cold against my ear when Larry spoke. I bit my lip and thanked the man for his guide to the Diamond Exchange and the list of Johnny's cop mates. Before he could ask, I admitted both seeds had borne fruit. Larry lied about being happy to help. Larry didn't understand happy, but even at this distance I could hear him tallying up the payback. Larry understood debt. I decided to increase mine.

There was just one more little favor I had to ask. I gave him as much as I could about Kate Barnum. I needed to know more. I needed to know why she was dumped from the *Times*. I wanted the inside skinny on her husband's suicide. I needed to know about any dirt, about anything that could hurt or stop her. Larry didn't respond immediately, but I could swear I heard his fangs clicking against the phone. Larry didn't have to ask why. He understood about blackmail and painting people into corners. Some people painted corners of their own.

Kate Barnum's number came quickly enough to my finger. I'd just dictated it to Larry. I got in half a ring before her smoky voice interrupted.

"Your hand surgically attached to the phone?"

"God," she coughed, "I wish I could be so witty. Do you think you could teach me?" Barnum moved on without waiting for my answer. "I got prelims on the deceased bird collector. Want it now or in person?" This time she waited.

"Give me the basics now and we can get particular later," I spoke, expecting the dead woman to have; '. . . some kinda funny name. Something biblical. Andrella, maybe.' That's what O'Toole had prepared me for. It's not what I got.

"Carlene Carstead. 1422 General Lee Boulevard, Biloxi, Mississippi. Forty-four years of age. Unmarried. No children. Assistant manager Dixieland Pig and Whistle, 2001 Delta Avenue, Biloxi . . ."

She droned on like that for some time. I'm not sure when I stopped paying attention. My mind was racing fast enough to lap itself. I tried recalling the dead woman's made-up orange face and her self-possessed tone of voice when asking for Johnny Blue. Somehow my recollections of her didn't add up to the deep south. South Brooklyn maybe, but not the deep south.

"Do you have a place of birth down there?" I shouted into the mouthpiece.

"Wait . . . Yeah, right here; Baptist and Saviour Hospital, Baton Rouge, Louisiana, 4/1/45. Why?" Barnum had picked up on my frantic curiosity for a fact which shouldn't have mattered much.

"Nothin'," I did my best stage yawn.

"Nothing my ass, Klein," the reporter didn't care much for my acting.

"Speaking of your ass . . ." I injected, trying another tack.

"Later. Tonight around eight?" she agreed too readily, figuring she'd have more success with me in person.

"Eight it is. Make me up a copy of your little fact sheet. Okay?"

"It'll be here. Klein!" she screamed, sensing me about to hang up.

"Yeah?" I pulled the phone back to my ear.

"What do you suppose a glorified grocery clerk from Biloxi was doing in Sound Hill, Long Island, New York on Christmas Eve? And what do you suppose she did to make someone mad enough at her to blow an access road through her skull and then pave it with golden feathers? Klein," she paused, waiting for an answer that wasn't forthcoming. "You're not the only mathematician in town. Pretty soon the whole neighborhood's gonna be working on this equation. I've already started putting some twos and twos together myself."

"And what'd'ya get?" I played along.

"A headache. But my best hunches come on the heels of headaches. Work fast, Klein," Barnum's voice dropped into a more serious octave. "I don't think we're alone in this anymore." I listened to her phone rattle back into its cradle.

I waited for a dial tone and punched up long distance info. Both numbers were listed. They would be. I knew that. Now the ugly part would follow; the scamming, the half-truths, the things that I'd fooled myself I'd left behind. I felt an old need. I brewed some coffee.

I liked coffee less these days. Maybe it was just less important. When I did insurance work, coffee kept me company. When I was an ambulance chaser's best friend, trailing broken necks to make certain they were wearing their braces, most of my blood was bagel-shop java. When I had to pretend about who I was and what I wanted and why, coffee straightened my face, stiffened my spine, told some of the better lies. And when the deception was done,

I could piss my spent muscle into the empty cup it'd come in. Now this stuff with Johnny had brought it all back; the lies, the scamming and the coffee.

If they could swat a ball around like they bounced my call back and forth, the folks at Baptist and Saviour Hospital in Baton Rouge, Louisiana would have one hell of a volleyball squad. One thing you have to give those Cajuns though, they were polite about fucking up. At least I got to the office I wanted without speaking to any patients.

"Patient Records, Marie Antoinette Gilbeau speakin'. How can we help y'all today?" a voice as bright as the noonday sun wanted to know.

"Hey, yo, Marie Antoinette," I laid on the Brooklynspeak thicker than the walls of a fallout shelter. "Let 'em eat cake, right baby?"

"I suppose," her tone darkened at the repetition of a bad joke she'd probably heard every day of her life since she was three.

"Sorry 'bout dat," I confessed. "Forgive an old cop for his stupidity?" The lie came to my lips easy enough.

"Cop!" Miss Guilbeau seemed impressed. "Y'ain't no local lawman. Dat tone a your's 'bout as Yankee as dey come."

"Sharp, baby. Very sharp. You gotta good ear," I complimented, noting to myself that her dialect and mine weren't that different. "Detective Bob Bosco, New York City Police, Missing Persons." I left it there. If the hunch I was playing had any merit, she'd supply the momentum.

"I gotta go have my palm read or sometin'. You de third person from New York I spoke wid dis week." My hunch had merit. "Seems some woman born down dis way been murdered up north. Cryin' shame, de value a life dese days."

"Sickening." No need to lie about that.

"Ain't it? You wouldn't be callin' bout de same woman, would ya?"

"Carlene Carstead, born 4/1—"

"Dat's her, sure 'nough," Marie cut me off. "April Fools Baby." I hadn't realized, but Miss Antoinette's observation was quite right. "I imagine it's cruel a me to say, but someone's been playin' an awful joke wid dat poor baby's memory."

"I'm sorry, Marie, but you just lost me," I admitted. "What baby? We're talkin' about a woman in her forties."

"Maybe *you* are, but dat dead woman ya got up dere ain't de same one got born in dis here hospital. "No sir," my phone pal proclaimed indignantly.

"How's dat?" I pushed her for an explanation I'd already guessed at.

"Now I ain't a curious Cajun by nature," Marie Antoinette offered her disclaimer, "but dem two phone calls got to workin' on my mind. I did some back checkin' and ya know what I found?"

"What'd'ya find?" I fed her the line she was hungry for.

"De Carlene Carstead dat was brought ta God's green earth in dis hospital was pronounced D.O.A. here five years later," she paused to give her words a chance for maximum impact. "I pulled a copy a de death certificate myself. Death by drowning. I read de whole report. Playin' wid her olda sista down ta Ponsichatchi Creek. Sista was revived. Ya know, Detective Bosco, y'all don't seem very surprised by any dis," the not-so-curious Cajun noted with a ring of suspicion in her voice.

"I said you was a sharp one. It's all de years on de job," I confided. "God it wears ya down. Sometimes I gotta pinch myself ta make sure I still got feelins."

"I know how it is," she commiserated. "Doctors 'round here say de same tins 'bout what dey doin'." Then, switching gears, the former queen of France asked: "Ya gonna find who's playin' dis awful joke wid dat sweet baby's memory?"

"I'm gonna try, Marie Antoinette. I am gonna try."

"Ya find out. I gotta sense 'bout it dat ya will."

"One more item," I threw in before our farewells. "Can ya name the other people who called about Carlene?"

"Sure can. First one was a woman reporter name a Kate Barnum. Second was a Detective Mickelson from out your way."

"Does anyone else besides us know the truth about Carlene?" I wondered.

"No Detective Bosco, uh uh, nobody."

"If ya want me ta find out who de joker is, let's keep it dat way. It's our secret for now," I spoke it like an oath.

"Our secret," she repeated.

With that vow and a few bonding good-byes, our conversation ended. I poured some fresh coffee down into my suddenly empty soul. It wasn't the lying and scamming that hurt me so much, but rather the dark pride I took in it. I thought about the price I paid for denial. I thought about my contempt for Lawrence Solomon Feld and about how you hate things in other people you can't bear about yourself. I thought about confirming my hunches and dialing the Dixieland Pig and Whistle in Biloxi. Oddly, I thought about Kate Barnum's smoky breath and her appetite for hurt. My chirping phone prevented further progress into the abyss. Sometimes, I liked the phone.

It was MacClough wanting me to stop by the Scupper. He wanted help with this or that. Some table had to come up from downstairs. I should come in via the alleyway. It wasn't an unusual request. Speech came slowly to me. I was like a stroke victim struggling with aphasia, groping for words and a tone which had once come to my lips without thought. It was one thing to scam a stranger over two thousand miles of phone line. It was quite another to fool your best friend who just happened to be an ex-detective. Johnny didn't seem to notice my aphasia and promised me a week of drinks for my trouble. I put down the phone, smiling with dark pride.

Penelope and Ulysses

Smack! A fist, a 2 × 4 or a low flying aircraft made square contact with my unsuspecting face. I went down like a sack of farm stand potatoes, blood filling my mouth even before my cut lips could kiss the floor of Johnny's back room. Exploding tears burned my blind eyes. Streams of unrestrained mucous gushed out of my flattened nose onto the floor, over my mustache and into the wet jungle of my beard.

All at once the world was deafeningly quiet and quietly deafening. The silence was broken soon enough. Stabbing rings of pain bounced like a pendulum between my eardrums as my breakfast coffee and chunks of semidigested twelve grain toast rocketed up out of my stomach, through my bloody mouth and onto the old wood floor. The sour smell of my own guts brought up whatever was left.

I felt, more than heard, heels moving along the floor beside me. Suddenly the pain in my head moved downstairs. My ribs flexed with the kick, but whatever air had managed to stick in my lungs through the facial assault and vomiting, escaped. I tensed the parts of me that still worked, readying for a follow-up kick. None came, that I remember. Only blackness. Only blackness came.

I might have been there a week or three centuries. I don't know. Maybe it just felt like forever. Cold water washed down over me, bits of jagged ice pinging off my sore neck. The chilly water resurrected more than simply me. The smell of my stale throw-up rose up like a rotting corpse from the New Testament to tug at my intestines. The dry retching seemed almost worse than the original attack. Almost.

Johnny MacClough, dressed in fog and holding a bucket, stood now just before me. A second freezing shower rained down, the ice pecking at my goose bumpy skin like the sharp beaks of angry birds. The empty bucket fell. I held an arm up to him that he should help me stand. Oh, he helped me stand all right. He twisted my coat and shirt collars up in his hard fingers and pulled my face to his. I could see my distorted reflection in a stainless steel counter over MacClough's shoulder. I cringed. Even through the fog and cobwebs and distortion, I could see I was a mess. I thought it an odd time to discover vanity. The thought made me smile. The smile caused the fresh scabs on my lips to split.

"What's so funny, Klein?" Johnny seemed unnerved by my inappropriateness.

"My face, Johnny. My face," I gasped as my tender ribs scolded me for speaking. MacClough turned his still foggy visage away from my sour breath.

"Did you really think you could go to my ex-partners behind my back and not have me find out about it? Did you?" He tightened his grip.

"We live in hope, MacClough," I smiled some more. "I guess one of 'em called you about our chat."

"More than one," he shook his head sadly. "You're my friend, Klein. Why you snoopin' around behind my back about things that don't concern you?"

"If it concerns you, MacClough, it concerns me."

"Not this, Klein. Not this time." He loosened his hold, but not completely.

"Back in Brooklyn, friendship and loyalty had nothin' to do with pickin' and choosin' your spots. I also don't recall havin' my friends kick the shit outta me." That was all the heroic speech I could muster.

"Stay out of this, Klein," MacClough looked me in the

eyes and and released his grip. "You can't help me. Stay out."

I stepped back and walked around MacClough into the empty barroom. It was still an hour till the opening bell. My hands held what was left of my ribs together. They made a lousy patch. Most of the fog in my head had lifted, leaving only a migraine as a residue of its visit. I waited for Mac-Clough to follow. He did not. He would not.

"I know about her, Johnny, about who Carlene Carstead wasn't," I shouted through the door, not certain my sparring partner was still back there to hear me. "I know who she was to you," I paused waiting for him to stir. I might've waited forever. I took up again: "Ya know, MacClough," I got conversational; loud, but conversational, "I'm no stud at crossword puzzles, but even I couldn't trip over my own dick on this one. Down or across, it spells 'Witness Protection Program,'" I finally gave voice to the hunch I'd been playing all morning.

Still, there was no answer. Outside, beyond the windows, brass-handled doors and neon beer signs, a winter fishing boat blew a mournful horn for some nautical reason beyond my citified comprehension or maybe just to protest the long hush of winter. But its protest had come too late. Christmas Eve gunfire had already broken that long silence.

"There's some stuff, alotta stuff, I haven't worked out yet," I continued my one-way discussion with the walls. "I don't know who she rolled over on or when. Christ, MacClough, I don't even know her real name. But something made her come outta hiding, something made her come looking for Johnny Blue. What was it?" I paused to give space for an answer that would not fill it.

"There's a stiff buried in Dugan's Dump," I tried a new tack. "It's wearin' a gold and onyx pinky ring. But maybe you know about that already. I figure he's—sorry—he *was* the shooter. Maybe you figured that, too. Maybe you planted him there. Why don't we talk about it, MacClough?

Come on." Again nothing. "Listen, I'm not the only one interested in this. Soon, the whole neighborhood'll be working on the puzzle," I paraphrased Kate Barnum's warning.

This time I gave him a pause pregnant enough to have two sets of twins. I was willing to wait. My ribs were not so patient. I dragged my coat sleeve across my face, smearing the cracked leather with scarlet-laced mucous, bitter tears and sweat from the pain. I poured myself a sip of stout to wash away the pasty vomit coating in my mouth.It didn't work and the sweet, pungent flavor of the syrupy brew made me want to puke again.

I popped a lonesome quarter into the jukebox, punched up three numbers and started back toward the alley and the front seat of my car. Patsy Cline was singing the second line of "Crazy" by the time the back room door slammed behind me. MacClough hadn't moved. He just stood there blank-faced and cold-eyed, unmoving but probably not unmoved. I wanted to say something to him, but the ripe odor of my thrown-up breakfast wouldn't let me. I ran past him and fumbled with the exit door handle.

"Stay out of it, Klein," MacClough muttered over my shoulder, reaching around me and pulling the door open to the fresh, freezing air. "By the time anyone else puts things together, my business will be done."

Business! What's he talking, business? Murder wasn't business. Murder was murder no matter how you dressed it up. I'd worry about that later. For now, I was preoccupied with folding myself into the driver's seat and cursing the day I met John Francis MacClough. After the drive began, the target of my disdain switched to manual transmissions. On the journey to the hospital, my ribs made certain to point out every bump, pothole and road hazard. Every fucking one!

A great feature of eastern Long Island is the less tainted attitude of its health care professionals. Unlike the "if it's not a gunshot wound above waist, sit down, shut up and wait your turn" attitude which prevails at city hospitals, local trauma units will treat the non-terminal without a notarized letter from a clergyman certifying you have valid health insurance, and you won't even have to wait half as long as Penelope did for Ulysses to see a physician.

I had mixed feelings about my doctor. He was male. That was good because I didn't feel obliged to suck in my gut, which might have killed me, or to flirt. On the other hand, flirting in my current state would've been a real challenge. The doctor was young. That meant his education was still fresh and his techniques current. Unfortunately, his only application of those techniques might have involved lab cadavers that tended not to complain or litigate.

His nameplate indicated he was Jewish. That was, unless Steven Cohen had suddenly become a popular moniker in the Christian world. Oh, did I mention, he was wearing a yarmulke? I could be so observant. Normally, a doctor's religion didn't move me, but today I had a question.

"That was some nasty fall you took, Mr. Klein," Dr. Cohen muttered sarcastically, reaching around my back to grab the roll of tape. "Lucky they're only bruised. There!" he patted down the edge of the tape with equal amounts pride and aplomb. "In a few weeks they'll be like new. As for your nose . . ." he referred back to the X-ray, "it's fine, but you may wake up tomorrow with a black eye or two."

"Assuming I ever get to sleep," I slapped the binding about my ribs and immediately regretted the gesture.

"I see your point."

"Hey Doc," my smile surprised him, "I got kinda an odd question for you."

"Ask away, Mr. Klein," Dr. Cohen liked questions.

"How good are you with the Torah?"

"That *is* the oddist question I've been asked today," he smiled back, self-conscously adjusting his skullcap. "I'm fair. Why?"

"I'm a freelance writer and I'm researching a story on the flight of European Jews to Palestine after the war." Hey, it wasn't a total lie. I was a writer and I figured my approach would hook him. "Anyway, two sources of mine have mentioned a little girl who escaped from Auschwitz and made it to Palestine entirely on her own. Unfortunately, they can't remember her name exactly and I can't print the story without confirmation."

"It sounds quite amazing," Cohen admitted, his eyes as wide as silver dollars, "but what does my familiarity with the Torah have to do with any of this?"

"Patience, Doc. Patience." We both laughed at my inadvertent pun. "I'm getting to that. One of my sources swears she had a strange name, something biblical, something like Andrella. I don't know. I guess I'm just grasping at straws now."

Cohen started pacing, scratching at his hairless chin and rubbing the back of his neck. "Andrella, Andrella," he mouthed over and over, "Andrella." He stopped pacing: "Sorry, Mr. Klein. I'm drawing a blank, but I can check up on it and get back to you."

"Thanks, Doc, I'd really appreciate that." We shook hands. "And thanks for patching me up."

He told me it was no trouble at all, suggested that I come see him in a week and gave me something for the pain we both knew I was going to have. He warned me to take it easy and apologized for his coming up with zero on the girl's name. He assured me he'd get my number off the hospital report and that he'd call if his sources could deliver a name. He shook my hand and shook his head. Dr. Cohen didn't like not knowing answers. This was going to eat at him.

A butterball of a nurse in old-fashioned whites, a silly hat and elastic hose with enough tensile strength to support a small office building cleaned me up a bit, helped put me back together and gave me half a roll of Certs for my breath. I winked at her. She liked that. She escorted me to the exit at no extra charge. From here to the car I would have to fly solo.

"Mr. Klein!" Dr. Cohen came sprinting after me, one hand holding his yarmulke against the wind. "Mr. Klein!" I stopped to let him catch me and to catch my breath. "I don't know if it's the name you're looking for," he was gasping for air himself. "Too much time trying to keep everyone else in shape," the young doctor held his heart.

"The name, Doc," I put him back on course.

"Could it have been Azrael?" he wondered sheepishly, as if regretting the speaking of those words aloud.

"I guess it could've been. It's odd. It's biblical-sounding," I was non-committal and just this side of unenthusiastic. The fact was, I didn't know.

"No," he kicked disappointedly at the ground, "it wouldn't be that. I don't even know why I suggested it."

"Educate me, Doc. Why wouldn't it have been her name?"

"Azrael, Mr. Klein, is the angel of death. Would any parent name his or her child after the angel of death?"

"In this world, who knows?" I threw up my hands and almost collapsed in pain. "But I suppose you're right, Doc. Nice try, anyway. Thanks."

He left me without a farewell, walking back to the hospital like the Mighty Casey walking back to the dugout after the third strike. Doctor Cohen was a little less familiar with failure than myself. That was good for him.

Once folded in, I sat in the driver's seat for a few minutes thinking about the angel of death. I thought about the angel's trail I'd been following lately, about the stiff in the dump and the little drowned girl with the stolen name. I thought about the dead woman in orange make-up and mink. And, I thought, if her name wasn't Azrael, God, it should have been.

And She Did

"You look like shit," Kate Barnum noted before I had both of my legs through the door of the scavenged old whaling ship.

"The best part is, I get to feel worse than I look," I winked, easing myself into her age-shredded sofa. "Got a beer to wash down my pain killers with?"

"Sure." She ambled barefoot into the kitchen and reappeared holding a glass mug smeared with fingerprints on the outside and full of unnamed beer within. "How'd it happen? And don't tell me you fell into an uncovered washing machine."

"Nah. If that happened, I'd be dead. Can't swim a stroke." I got guilty quiet thinking about a little girl floating face down in Ponsichatchi Creek. Sometimes it's not funny. What you think about, I mean.

Barnum mistook my change of expression for bad beer. "The beer sour?"

"No. Just everything else."

She lit a butt and nuzzled up next to me, her free hand falling carelessly onto my chest. I nearly passed out when it landed.

"Ribs," I coughed out.

"Sorry. Christ, you really are in bad shape. I thought the black eyes were just a fashion statement!" the reporter snickered nervously. "You must be getting close. Someone warn you off?"

"Yeah."

"Who?"

"Next question." I sat up again, breathing as normally as a man could with a hundred yards of tape around his middle.

"MacClough, huh." Barnum lit up the room with her self-satisfaction.

"You *are* good."

"I didn't get to where I was by being dull-witted, Klein."

"Yeah," I agreed, "but how'd ya get to where you are now?"

"Next question." It was her turn to look like a swallow of bad beer. We were even.

"Do you still have access to the *Times* morgue?" I wondered.

"Not officially. Why?"

"You're not Jewish, Barnum, so stop answering my questions with questions. Yes or no?"

"Yes," she acquiesced.

"Go back twenty-five years and work—"

"Twenty-five years!"

"And work forward," I continued. "You're lookin' for a mob trial in which a woman turns state's evidence and then goes underground."

Kate pulled a bottle of house brand bourbon out from under the kidney-shaped coffee table and took a warm-up swallow. When she was warmed up, she took another.

"You want to give me any details or am I going to have to stay in the morgue for twenty years just looking?" she queried with as much enthusiasm as a pig for a ham sandwich.

"Don't get so excited. One thing is you won't have to look that far forward. The envelope is twenty-five to twenty years ago. It's the only time frame that fits. Secondly, I'm pretty sure the woman's name was Azrael." I wasn't certain at all, but I *was* getting pretty comfortable with lying. "Might've been a nickname. I don't know."

"Azrael?"

I spelled it for her.

"Not much to go on," she yawned and took another swig. The cheap stuff was tasting like Wild Turkey by now.

"It's enough." I tamped out her cigarette to underline by two words.

"Let's fuck, Klein," she changed gears and subjects and removed her sweatshirt.

"Christ," I laughed uncomfortably, "I wish you'd just get to the point." I don't know what it is exactly. Maybe men are unnerved by women who not only think like they do, but who give voice to their thoughts. "Sorry," I ran a fingernail along the tape ridges about my ribs. "Besides, you play too rough."

"Just come with me, baby," she helped me out of my seat, her left nipple brushing my cheek. "I'll do all the work."

And she did. Most of it, anyway.

Now we were just lying there, sleepless and lonely on her smoky sheets in the dark; the absence of love robbing the room of breathable air. Even before she could finish taking what I had to give, I could feel the emptiness creep in the window like poison gas. In the absence of love, consummation is the cruelest part of desire. Barely able to make out her shape in the blackness and gas, I wondered if she'd simply gotten used to it. I never have.

"Do you know what question couples forever wonder about but never ask until it's too late?" Barnum spoke into the night.

"No," I answered, somehow relieved that she felt the absence, too.

"Where did it go? That's what they ask. Where did it go?"

And I did not respond. What was there to say, anyway? In any case, I was in no shape to look any harder at myself than I was already. She got up to find the bathroom and the bottle and a pack of cigarettes. I also think she went to take a look.

Magic Trick

My black eyes had just about finished their technicolor journey through the contusion spectrum. Their deep purple stage was definitely my favorite. I looked good in dark colors. As for my ribs. . . They were still sore, but it now took more than the brush of a careless hand to set me into convulsions. I decided to skip my follow-up visit with Doc Cohen until the painkillers ran out. MacClough and I were avoiding a rematch by avoiding each other. We both knew I couldn't leave things alone, but hey, stuff happens. Right?

Kate Barnum was splitting her time between two newspapers. Her articles in the *Whaler* concerning subtle changes in the local zoning ordinance were right on, but about as compelling as a compost heap. Covering this kind of stuff would kill her way before the butts and the booze. I could almost understand her desperation. Barnum's spare moments were spent digging at the *Times;* unofficially, of course, and without result.

I was sitting at the word processor watching the eleventh snowfall of the winter. Eleven stuck in my head because that was one more page than my short story about the Japanese contained. That's how many pages it had two weeks ago. That's how many pages it was going to have. I'd been making lots of lists lately of writers I'd never be. I caught myself praying for the phone to ring. Sometimes prayers get answered.

"This Klein?" the man's vaguely familiar voice wanted to know.

"This Klein. You Jane." I took a weak shot a humor.

"Huh?" My shot missed. "Funny man. Real funny." Johnny's ex-partner Terence O'Toole lashed out scornfully. "You remember me, funny man?"

"I remember you, O'Toole. I guess you're callin' about Johnny."

"Yeah, I been thinking about him and that bitch."

"What you been thinking about 'em?" I tried moving things along.

"You remember where I live?" The ex-cop was in a nasty mood.

"I remember."

"Get here. I got something to sell you." he laughed uncomfortably.

"What about the snow?"

"Fuck the snow. And hey, Klein, I'm almost dry. Bring me something for my throat. Maybe I'll knock a few bucks off the price," the old giant burped into my ear.

"One thing O'Toole," I didn't let him hang up.

"What?"

"The girl's name. Was it Azrael?"

"You been doing your homework, Klein," I could hear him smile. "Yeah, that was the Jew cunt's name," he stuck the verbal knife in and twisted it. "It's good that you done your homework. It'll make our business easier. Be here soon!"

I got there, but it wasn't soon. Old Volkswagens don't like the snow. I played my one cassette of British Invasion hits twice. It might've had time for a third go around, but I couldn't stand to hear "Pictures of Matchstick Men" again. Like most things in my VW, the fast forward and rewind buttons hadn't worked in a decade. I kept pulling the new fifth bottle of Murphy's Irish out of the sack, but no combination of bad traffic, bad weather, bad ribs and bad music could make me take a sip.

O'Toole's block was beehive busy with snow day kids

hitting up their neighbors for snow shoveling money. In one form or another every driveway and every inch of sidewalk on the street had been dug out or cleared. No, not every driveway, not every inch. O'Toole's driveway was still a field of beaten egg whites and his sidewalk was invisible under the white snow. I didn't like it. I don't know why. I just didn't.

There were two sets of footprints leading up the steps to the old cop's door. One set was small and irregular. Probably the result of a neighbor kid fighting the accumulation, looking for snow removal work. The other set was widely spaced and deep and made by an adult foot. I'd guess a man's foot, but what the fuck did I know from footprints. The bigger prints had come first. I could tell that much. More snow had re-accumulated in their cavities than in the small prints. I thought about the print Azrael had left in the snow outside the Rusty Scupper and then rang O'Toole's bell.

He didn't answer and he never would. He woud never drink the Murphy's or throw a shot glass at his dead son's photo. He'd never again call anyone nigger or Jew cunt or spic or dot head. He'd just rot in a grave like everyone he hated.

I opened the storm door and put some light pressure on the front door. It fell back at my touch. The hallway was dark. Not the black dark of night, but the beige-brown shadows of frayed canvas shades and deep green wallpapers that only the blind would not find depressing. I slid along the hallway expecting to find death in the kitchen. I was not disappointed.

The giant lay on his belly, head away from me, legs twisted, disheveled and still. He looked like a magic trick that someone had forgotten to finish. I flipped on the chandelier, but somehow the room didn't brighten much. There'd be no profit in checking for signs of life, so I didn't. Funny thing was, I couldn't immediately make out what killed him. On my hands and knees now, I looked for clues in his glassy, opened eyes that reminded me of those on the freshly dead fishes in Sheepshead Bay.

There was blood; a hint, a trickle where his lumberjack shirt over lapped his cheap belt. When I lifted him up a bit, the hint became a flood. I stepped out of its path. He'd been belly-shot at close range. I couldn't say how many times. A shirt full of scarlet goo sort of obscures things. I patted him down, checking for whatever it was he was trying to sell me. Unless it was an empty pocket, he didn't have it on him. For a flicker I considered the possibility that he was bluffing, but I pushed that thought away. O'Toole wasn't the type.

There would be cops. I couldn't sidestep them, but I made another call first. The phone rang a few times before someone picked up. The voice at the other end was one I hadn't heard for awhile.

"MacClough's Rusty Scupper."

"Johnny?" I asked out of nerves more than anything.

"How's the ribs?" he wondered matter-of-factly.

"I'll live," I answered, unconsciously running my hand along the tape beneath my shirt. "You know where your old partner O'Toole's house is?"

"Why?" McClough's tone cooled considerably with one syllable.

"I'm there right now. I think you should join me."

"Put that old donkey on the line," the bar owner demanded.

"Let's just say he's indisposed, Johnny," I offered sardonically, looking down at the dead man. "I'll wait for you." I hung up.

I sat down in the chair I'd parked in during my last trip here. I didn't like the fact that Johnny didn't need directions to the house. O'Toole and Johnny didn't strike me as two guys who would've kept in touch. I asked the lifeless giant about that. He didn't answer. I asked him what it was he was trying to pawn off on me and where it might be hiding? He was as mum as the fishes in Sheeps-head Bay or the ones on the Scupper's walls. I got tired of not getting answers, so I stopped asking questions.

I wanted to do a cursory search of the dead cop's joint, but couldn't risk how that might look to the detectives when they showed. And they would show. Besides, I didn't know what I was hunting for. I just looked around from my seat and saw what there was to see in the diffuse brown light. That took a quick fifteen seconds, give or take ten.

I caught myself staring at the ornately framed portrait of O'Toole's elephant-eared kid in military dress. Something about it bothered me. I thought it might be the pain in the dead kid's expression, but no. That had been there the first time I'd seen the photo, the first time O'Toole had hurled his shot glass at it. I kept staring.

Bang! It hit me, but with a little less force than Mac-Clough's right fist or left shoe. There *was* something askew, but not with the photo itself. No. The glass that'd covered it previously was out of the frame, missing. Maybe it meant nothing. Maybe O'Toole's shot glass aim had improved and he'd hit his target once before passing from this earth. Or maybe it meant the glass had been purposely removed to clear some space for storage behind the dead boy's photo.

Before dissecting the frame, I ran my fingertips over the glass-free photo. I could feel there was more behind that dead Marine's expression than just pain. The contents poured out of the frame easily enough. Sandwiched in between the blackened cardboard backing and the snap of O'Toole's dead son were some curious odds and sods. There was a brittle yellow newspaper clipping, a list of phone numbers (some in pencil, faded and smudged; Some in pen, bright and recent) and a couple of other photographs.

There was one old Polaroid shot of Azrael and a young, uniformed John Francis MacClough taken at some garish and probably long since bankrupted restaurant. They held hands across a Peter Max printed tablecloth. Johnny was mugging for the camera. The girl's soul and smile were fixed on the man holding her hand. There was a head shot of just the girl. The lifeless gray hair I'd seen tucked under the ratty mink was once chestnut brown with auburn highlights in the sun. It was thick. God, it was thick; the kind of hair a man could lose a hand in, the kind of hair that came from God and not from any bottle. The dead eyes I'd seen searching the cloudy Christmas Eve sky were yellow-green crystals two decades ago. Her lips were just this side of thick and her lashes were sleek, dark feathers. Hanging against the tanned, freckled skin of her chest was a familiar heart-shaped diamond pendant. The heavy orange make-up of middle age was absent. Maybe she had less to hide back then. She was, as its said in Brooklyn, a woman to die for. Some probably had.

Behind the snap of Azrael came another photo almost identical to the one of Johnny and the girl; same restaurant, maybe even the same table. Only in this one, the chestnut-haired girl held hands with a very different man. The stud in Johnny's shoes was modelishly handsome with curled brooding lips, sable hair, cold black eyes and a chiseled chin with a cleft that could hold a pearl. He did not mug for the camera. He would not have to. The camera loved him. Two things about Azarel were markedly different in this Polaroid; the orphaned heart was missing as was the love and admiration in her eyes.

The last photo was recent. It was oversized, satin-finished and lacked the white border of both older pictures. Unfortunately, the photographer and his subject had botched the job. The picture was blurry, overexposed, done with the wrong speed film and taken from too far away. Other than that it was perfect. This masterpiece was a side shot of a woman between the ages of twenty and thirty getting into a car. What car? What woman? I couldn't tell you. But if this was the best shot on the roll, I'd hate to see the rest.

The yellow newspaper clipping had been cut out sans date but the print said that it came from the *Times*. The words told me mostly what I had expected. Mostly. The article recapped the events surrounding the trial of a certain mob figure. It seems that the government had failed to prove its case in spite of the compelling testimony of its star witness—Azrael Esther Wise, born Esther Wiseman in Brooklyn, N.Y. on V-E Day 1945—the paramour of the defendant's oldest son. Nothing terribly enlightening here. I'd guessed at the greater part of this anyhow. The one surprise came in the letters that spelled the defendant's last name: Gandolfo.

That's right, Gandolfo. Gandolfo, as in Dante "Don Juan" Gandolfo. Gandolfo, as in Larry Feld's biggest client. The trial had been that of Dante's father, Roberto "The Boot" Gandolfo, and the star witness had been Dante's girl. Sometimes the world is too small a place to suit me, much too small a place.

I flipped back to the photo of Azrael and the brooding male model holding her hand. Then I squeezed my eyes shut and recalled the blowup in Larry Feld's office of himself, Mike Wallace and Dante Gandolfo. Add a few years, a few pounds, a little gravity, some salt to the black pepper of his hair and there'd be a match. O'Toole had told me that Johnny's girl had been a wiseguy's toy. Christ, MacClough could really pick them. But even here, with a bloody stiff at my feet, I couldn't blame Johnny. In twenty-year-old pictures, she could make you want her. Believe me. She could. I wondered what kind of world it was that turned her into the orange-faced loser I found eating canary on Christmas Eve.

Before burying my new-found booty in my pocket, I spread the old news clipping out on the dead man's table. It looked strange unfolded like that. What I mean to say is that most of the article had been neatly scissored or razored out, but one of the edges was rough, torn, uneven. The tear seemed fresh. Fresher, at least, than the cut edges. Someone had recently removed a piece of the puzzle and I didn't have time to look for it. I heard steps crunching up the snow on the front steps.

"Dead?" Johnny asked, already knowing the answer.

"Quite dead."

MacClough put his knee in the pool of drying blood and lifted the body just as I had. He shook his head and let the corpse back down: "Belly shot with a twenty-two. Three, maybe four times. He let the killer get awfully close to him. Asshole."

I didn't disagree.

"Call the cops?" MacClough wanted to know.

"Not yet."

"Why not?"

"I figured we had a lot to talk about first," I prodded.

"Is that what you figured?" Johnny was just full of questions.

"Uh huh," I could be so articulate.

"Then you need help with your figuring," the wary ex-cop advised. "We don't have anything much to discuss."

This sparring was giving me a bellyache and making me remember my sore ribs. I wasn't much in the mood and I was getting pretty fucking tired of digging for every answer and then trying to decipher it like a hieroglyph. I laid it out for him much as I had the brittle newsprint.

"Look Johnny," I slammed my fist on the table, "let's stop the cha-cha. Her name was Azrael Wise and she was Dante Gandolfo's property. Problem was, she didn't love him. She loved you. But 'Don Juan' wasn't an easy guy to walk away from, especially after she'd seen things. She'd seen the kinda things that get some people a half-dozen consecutive lifetimes in stir. She'd seen the kinda things that get other people to swallow bullets. Anyway, she rolled over on Dante's old man. I suspect with a big push from a chesty, rookie cop who was sure he knew what the right thing was," I cleared my throat. "Stop me when I get cold,"

He didn't stop me.

"So, with you pushing, she witnessed against Robby 'The Boot.' And that was that. Azrael was *persona non grata* everywhere on this planet murder could reach. She bid adieu to Johnny Blue, riding off into the sunset on the back of the Witness Protection Program. But the program wasn't so sophisticated then like it is now. Now they use fake social security numbers and fabricated identities. When Azrael went underground, they used the identities of people who didn't have much use for 'em anymore. You know, people like a little dead girl who drowned while her big sister watched," I was shouting now. "People with names like Carlene Carstead, for instance."

He still didn't stop me.

"You're in this shit, MacClough, up to your guilty nipples and I'm tryin' like hell to pull ya out. Don't even tell me ya don't want my help," I waved off any potential objection. "You're gettin' it.

"Now I know you didn't whack Azrael and I don't think you whacked Mr. Pinky Ring either. Ya might have, if you'd gotten the chance. I just don't think ya got that chance. Him," I shrugged at O'Toole's nearly forgotten body, "maybe he was squeezin' ya. Maybe ya had to quiet him. But even if ya didn't, you're gonna kill. I can smell it on ya like my father's cheap aftershave on Sunday mornings. I don't know that I could stop ya, but I figure to try."

He shook his head from side to side: "You still need help with your figuring."

"You help me," I pointed at him accusingly. "You help me make sense outta this. Why'd she come outta hiding after all these years? Christ, the old man wasn't even convicted and he's not head of the family anymore. The contract on her must've been colder than Candlestick Park in July. Why now, Johnny? Why now?"

"We got nothin' to talk about, Klein, except maybe the weather."

"Okay, MacClough, the cops are gettin' called," I moved for the phone.

"Yeah and so what happens?" the ex-detective seemed less nervous about the cops' arrival than the dead man at his feet.

"I'll talk a lot. I'll let them stop ya, if ya won't let me," my voice cracked as if puberty was late in arriving. "I'll tell 'em that you killed O'Toole. I'll tell 'em anything I have to."

"They won't listen," he yawned. "Here," he handed me the phone, "call."

"I can prove you withheld evidence," I took up his challenge and the phone. "In fact I bet you're carrying that evidence with you in the shape of a diamond heart. Try explaining that away."

The corner of his mouth twitched as a drop of sweat rolled off his upper lip. The granite cracked.

"You won't do that," MacClough fingered off the sweat. "You'll be hanging yourself. You were the one who lied to the cops. You were the one who held back the jewelry. All I have to say is I was holding the heart for you, that I didn't know where it came from or who it was for."

"You're wrong, Johnny. I'll do it. Whatever it takes. I'll do it." Puberty struck again. "When all is said and done, the stink that gets raised will be enough to warn anybody off."

"Why don't you just call my alleged victim and warn him straight out?" Johnny smirked sardonically.

"Because that'll make you a target. And that's the only thing I won't do. I don't want any killing with you on either side of the gun barrel," I shook my head no. "Why don't you just give it to the cops and let them take care of it."

"The cops!" MacClough's hearty laugh was lined in sadness. "The cops wouldn't be able to pin this on the Gandolfos with shoestring and bubblegum. I'm somewhat familiar with how both sides work. Anyway, even if they managed to make a case, the Gandolfos' whore mouthpieces would shoot it down before it ever got to trial. No, Klein, this is old business. My business."

I couldn't really dispute Johnny's arguments. He knew the cops and I knew the lawyer. We were at an impasse and the body at our feet wasn't going to keep forever. I called 911, gave my name and suggested the coroner be alerted. We waited.

At the distant squawking of sirens, John Francis spoke up: "When the locals show, play along with me. Play along and you'll get your answers."

"When?"

"You'll get your answers," he repeated, ignoring my schedule request. "But I can't let you stop me."

"Fair enough," I extended my hand for a shake.

He shook it and pulled my right ear close to his lips. "I loved her, Klein."

Lots of feet were crushing the snow on the stoop now. Fists knocked on the door and bells chimed like Big Ben with a sore throat. Discordant voices shouted, "Police. Open up." MacClough pushed me away, took out his detective's shield and started marching to the entrance. Halfway down the shadowed hall, he turned back to me.

"Christ, I really loved her," he shook his head. "Don't forget. Play along." He continued up the hallway.

Sure I was going to play along. Didn't Johnny know? I'd been playing along most of my life.

Polyester Suits, Dacron Shirts, Nylon Socks and Vinyl Shoes

I played along. I was still without answers, but I played along. God, it was scary to see the ease with which Mac-Clough manipulated the uniforms. Uniformed cops, in spite of their resentment and envy, can act awfully like novice priests in the presence of the Pope when presented with the gold and enamel of a detective's shield. They can't help themselves. From their first day on the job they shoot for that shield. They shoot for the day they can dress in polyester suits, dacron shirts, nylon socks and vinyl shoes. They shoot for the day when someone can kiss *their* rings. It's funny. It didn't seem to matter that Johnny was retired and that he was supposed to have returned the shield and that he was two counties removed from his former jurisdiction. It didn't seem to matter and he knew it.

The Suffolk Homicide detectives were considerably less impressed, but MacClough was light on his feet. Now it was his turn to kiss some ass and kiss some ring and genuflect till his knees got sore. This song and dance wasn't as much fun as watching Johnny control the uniforms, but it worked just as well. These guys seemed pretty receptive to our cock and bull story.

My words were just a variation on a theme. I was going to throw my buddy, John MacClough, a party celebrating five years of retirement. Unfortunately, I wasn't well acquainted with his old sleuthing pals. So, I was making the rounds of his ex-partners and such, trying to enlist their help. O'Toole was just one name on this list I had. We'd spoken once before and had agreed to meet soon. He'd called me this morning to say it was a good day for him. When I showed up, the door was open and he was dead. I guess I panicked a little and called MacClough. He came straight away and that's when I called the cops. Johnny stood firmly at my right shoulder throughout my telling, shaking his head in religious agreement.

We both knew the story would hold up. The phone records would show the O'Toole call to me and mine to Johnny. The times of our separate arrivals would check out. And, if the Suffolk detectives bothered checking on my party yarn, they'd find a half-dozen New York City cops who'd testify that I had, in fact, approached them with that concept. Things were going just swimmingly considering I'd just found my second body in as many months. But such smooth sailing has never been in my stars.

I recognized the belly even before its bearer was entirely through the front door. Detective Sergeant Mickelson shook a few hands, slapped a few backs and walked right up to me. He could see the consternation in my eyes. He liked that. I could see that in his.

"Well, well, Mr. Klein," he feigned surprise and shook my hand. "Palm's a little sweaty for such a cold day."

"Finding bodies sort of unnerves me."

"Shit, Klein, I thought you'd be getting pretty used to it by now," the fat detective needled. "If you were as good at finding crude oil as bodies, the fucking Arabs would go broke."

I decided to jump out of the hole he was digging me. "Yeah and if you were as good at police work as you are at eating, the world would be crime free."

"Okay, cocksucker," Mickelson put his face in mine, "let's hear this week's bullshit story."

He heard it. He didn't like it. But he wasn't going to like it anyway. That was his *schtick*.

"You're improving, Klein," Buddha belly complimented. "At least this time I can almost believe you. Who knows, by the time you find your next carcass maybe you'll be good enough to fool me."

"We live in hope." I smiled.

"You know, Klein, that broad you found on the train platform's got a real interesting biography," the enlightened detective switched gears and bodies.

"Really? No, I didn't know that."

"It's fascinating stuff," he prodded. "And you know what?"

"What?"

"When I'm done with it, it's gonna lead right to your friend's door," he pointed across the room at MacClough. "I feel it in my belly. And—"

"—your belly's never wrong," I cut him off and finished. "There's always a first time."

"Yeah," he agreed, "but this ain't it. I'm gonna tie this all together into one pretty little bundle. And when I do, your ass and his'll be tucked neatly inside."

"Thanks for the warning, Detective," I scratched my ass and yawned to cover the turmoil in my intestines. "Can I go now?"

"You can go," Mickelson granted my request. "Klein!" he called me back. "Isn't there anything you can tell me now? Maybe I can keep you clear of the fallout and soften your buddy's fall. No cop likes to see another cop . . . You know what I mean."

"I know," I shook my head that I understood. "Mickelson," I whispered in his ear, "go fuck yourself." I walked away before the fat man could react.

Mickelson was right. His fucking belly was right. All roads led to John Francis MacClough. I was taking one of those roads when an amused detective shooed me away.

MacClough was off limits to me currently. He was too busy entertaining the troops with old war stories from his days on the job to be bothered with the trivia that was me. I get interrogated and he gets laughs. Good thing I never labored under the illusion of fairness.

On my way out, the forensic team relieved me of some of my wardrobe; my green ramie sweater and motorcycle jacket. Nitrate tests again! I was pissed. It was too cold out for this crap. Last time the clothing had been Johnny's. The cops said it couldn't be avoided. I saw Mickelson where I'd left him, laughing at my predicament. That was better. Now I was getting laughs, too. Maybe life was fair. I smiled. I left.

Jackie Robinson and Babe Ruth

For a guy who was trying to convert himself from an insurance investigator into a writer, I sure didn't spend much time in libraries. I never had. I never would. It wasn't that I hated little index cards. Oh, I did hate them, but it went deeper than that. It wasn't that I didn't get the Dewey Decimal System. I didn't. It went back to sixth grade when I took two books—*The Jackie Robinson Story* and *The Babe Ruth Story*—that were months overdue and threw them down a sewer behind my elementary school. I didn't have the money to pay for the late charges nor did I have the courage to ask my folks for the bread. I almost asked Larry Feld, but decided the sewer maneuver would cost me less in the end. I hadn't had a public library card since. Guilt is a great mystery to me.

Like most of the older buildings in Sound Hill, the library bore a huge metal plaque on one of its flanks declaring it a sight of some historic importance. The Rusty Scupper had such a plaque. It had been a whalers' meeting hall. The library building had once housed the whale meat, blubber and oil collected by Conrad Dugan's fleet. Now it housed just so many copies of *Moby Dick*.

Once inside the old warehouse, I didn't bother with the pretense of fumbling about and looking lost. I went straight to the front desk. The woman there was fortyish, somber and busy reading *The Wasteland and Other Poems* by T.S. Eliot. Just some light and cheery stuff for a snowy winter's day. I wondered if her idea of romance was dissecting small woodland creatures. No, I decided, nothing that fluffy.

She wasn't a stranger to me nor I to her. In a village the size of Sound Hill, anonymity is just dreamed about. It's probably the only aspect of New York City life Sound Hillians envied. Sometimes, like now maybe, it was the one thing I missed.

"You're that Klein fellow," she snapped and pointed, laying T.S. to rest with respect. At least she didn't kiss the cover first. "You found the dead woman on Christmas Eve," she raised an eyebrow, noticing I was without jacket or sweater or proper shirt.

"That's me," I winked, "Miss . . . Emery," I read off the engraved, black laminate nameplate, trying to ignore my T-shirt as an issue.

"Miss Emery passed on when I was in high school," she tisked tisked me. "We keep that nameplate as a memorial to her years of dedicated service."

Ain't small town life a grand thing?

"Sorry, Ms. . ." I reached around the corners of my memory. Just because I knew her face didn't mean I knew her name, "Piper. Ms. Piper."

"*Miss* Piper," she fairly hissed.

I hadn't killed O'Toole, but a few more minutes of this and the next stiff Mickelson and I chatted over *would* be a product of my handiwork!

"Look, Miss Piper, I need some help," I pulled out the old newspaper clipping and laid it in front of her. "This is from the *New York Times* about twenty, twenty-five years ago—"

"It have anything to do with that murder?"

I almost asked which one, but realized she could only mean Azrael's.

"Could be," I winked again. I was a good winker. "Official stuff. Hush-hush," I put my index finger vertically across my lips.

"Why didn't you just say so?" Ms. Piper nearly flew out from behind her desk. "Come with me."

I had her. She was hooked. Secretly, everyone thinks they're Sherlock Holmes. I was kind of partial to Dr. Watson myself.

Out from behind the dark, burdensome desk, Miss Piper displayed a pert, gangly stride that would have been considered cute in her teens. Now it just seemed awkward. My secret Sherlock was pleasantly shaped, slightly bowed at the knees and a little long in the neck. Her face had never been called pretty by anyone besides her relatives, but no one had ever cowered in fear at the sight either. Her hair was mousy brown and wavy, falling here and there about her shoulders. Piper's eyes were dull copper buttons and the left one sort of drifted away from her nose. She was the type of woman I could just as easily sleep with as walk past in the street.

"Here we go," she beckoned me to sit before a blue-lighted screen. "All the issues of the *Times* are on these shelves. Your time-frame issues are in this group here. Let me show you how to work this thing." Piper plucked out a sheet of microfilm, placed it on a tray beneath the screen and expertly manipulated the print. "You try."

I tried, getting the hang of it rather quickly. She hung over my shoulder to make sure. I liked the way she smelled. God, I was easy.

"Good," Miss Piper patted my back. Maybe I was going to get a gold star. "We had a reporter on the *Times* once," she offered, her voice half full of pride. I couldn't be sure about the other half. "Do you know Kate Barnum?"

"No," I lied and played dumb. I was better at those things than winking.

"Are you certain you don't know her? She writes for the *Whaler* now."

"That's quite switch," I turned to Miss Piper.

"That's a kind way to put it, Mr. Klein." The other half of the librarian's voice was sounding kind of nasty.

"How would you put it, Miss Piper?"

"I would call it more of a fall than a switch. Yes," she seemed to be searching the ceiling for approval, "most decidedly a fall, a very big fall."

I tended to agree and fed her a few syllables of encouragement: "That's a shame."

"You *are* too kind." She was properly encouraged. "Kate Barnum has no one to blame but herself. The way she was with boys in school, it's no wonder her first husband kicked her right out. Drove her second husband to suicide. Now I'm no gossip . . ."

"Of course not," I pushed a tad harder. Why is it that the guilty always deny the obvious?

"Word in town was," Piper drew her cruel lips close to me, "the city police were trying to build a murder case against her. I don't think she did it though."

Yeah, sure she didn't believe it. Little Missy Piper sounded as convincing as a hungry leopard swearing off fresh-killed gazelle.

"So that's why the *Times* let her go?"

"I'm sure it had something to do with it. Her drinking too. But it was the Pulitzer Affair that did it," the gangly madame let that hang in the air for a minute before going on. "Apparently, Katy was a lock for the Pulitzer Prize a while back. But out of the blue, she goes to her editor and admits to faking some research and using some questionable sources. Imagine the embarrassment."

"Yeah, just imagine," I turned my back on Miss Piper. Suddenly, I wasn't liking the way she smelled. "Thanks for the help," I choked on my words.

"If there's anything else I can assist you with . . ." she hinted hopefully.

"One thing," I didn't turn around. "Would I be way off if I guessed that this Pulitzer thing happened within a year, one way or the other, of her husband's death?"

Miss Piper's answer was this: "Are you sure you don't know Kate Barnum?"

I didn't reply. I listened to her footsteps fade away.

This microfilm thing was pretty tedious work. I mean I liked newspapers, but this was total sensory overload. I knew it was getting to me when I began rummaging through Mets' boxscores from April of 1966. About two hours into the ordeal, I found the first articles relating to the trial. You know the kind of headlines; "Reputed Crime Boss Indicted," "Underworld Trial Set To Begin," "Government Witness Takes Stand Against Mr. Gandolfo," "Jury Sequestered," "Verdict In: 'Not Guilty'." I garnered only inconsequential details from these additional readings. Apparently, Roberto Gandolfo liked to take long siestas in the courtroom and the pressure of testifying made Azrael nauseous and faint. Not very earth-shattering stuff.

Eventually I came to the clone of the article I found behind the snapshot of O'Toole's deceased kid. And like I suspected there were accompanying pictures; the usual grainy, blurry, newspaper fare. There were headshots of the accused, their attorneys, the prosecuting attorney and of Azrael. Even in this photo you could see some of the life and beauty had already been bleached out of her. Azrael's face was bloated and her eyes were full of only surrender. And in those eyes I saw the makings of the dead woman I discovered in the snow on Christmas Eve. But there was nothing in these pictures to explain why they had been ripped away from O'Toole's copy. Maybe I just wasn't seeing the obvious. It wouldn't be the first time.

I rubbed my eyes, looked around and slipped the relevant sheets of microfilm into my pants. My ribs were probably sore, but my back hurt so much it was difficult to tell. I replaced the files, minus my deletions, and went for the door. Miss Piper had returned to her reading. When she stood to say her good-byes, I just waved her down, mouthed a silent thank-you and blew her an insincere kiss. Once outside, I removed the acetate sheets from my pants and thought about getting caught. I thought about Jackie Robinson and Babe Ruth. It's funny what you think about.

America's Dairyland

I drove by the Scupper. For the first time since I'd relocated the piece of Brooklyn that was myself, the pub was closed when it shouldn't've been. It's unscheduled darkness added to my jacketless chill. MacClough had always taken great pride in just being open according to the sign that hung in his door. A man of his word, John MacClough. A man to set your watch by. He'd never say any such thing, but you knew he wanted desperately for the world to believe it. I believed it.

We were an odd mix, Johnny and I. The superficial differences were obvious. He was older—in years anyway—an Irish Catholic, a veteran, a cop, a fighter. He'd seen Europe on maps and globes and the colleges he went to taught only hard knocks. His politics, like his stickball pitches, came overhand and from the right. Did I already mention that most of his hair follicles still functioned and that they seemed incapable of producing gray or silver growth?

But MacClough was an anchor to me, someone who remembered Brooklyn the way I remembered it; fireworks on Tuesday nights on the boardwalk, fifteen-cent subway rides, black and green police cars, chalkbox stickball, basketball on night-blackened courts with very bent rims and making out with high school girls on the abandoned lifeguard chairs at Brighton Beach. After our first year, MacClough and I didn't talk about home much. We didn't have to. We didn't want to. That Brooklyn no longer exists. And with each year, I wonder if it ever did. I know Johnny wonders, too.

125

To explain my relationship with MacClough, I usually tell this story: I lived in Wisconsin for a few years once. Why I lived there's not important to anyone but me and my heart. Well, anyway, things were going poorly for me in America's Dairyland and I'd been drinking too much. One night I found myself in some faceless bathroom in some nameless bar in Milwaukee. I'm pissing, head against the snotty tiles, when something taps my shoulder. "You went to PS 252, right?" I look up and there's this guy, whose name I still don't know, smiling at me like he's a crusader just found the Holy fucking Grail.

Meanwhile this guy's the same asshole Irish kid who used to mug us on Saturday mornings on the way home from synagogue. This is the kid who used to tie kids up with their prayer shawls and leave them hanging from No Parking signs. You know what I did? I put my dick back in my pants, pulled up my zipper and washed my hands. Then I gave that asshole Irish kid a great big hug and bought him a beer. Don't ask me why, but seeing that jerk there just then felt awfully like salvation. Johnny and I are sort of like that, I guess; a bit of the home we've lost forever. I can't reason it out for you. It's beyond that.

I pressed my face up against the Scupper's darkened window and wondered if MacClough was still busy entertaining the troops. I wanted answers. He'd promised them to me. But the Rusty Scupper's closed door was a broken promise. That's the funny thing about reliable people, it only takes one broken promise to shatter your faith in them. With people like Kate Barnum, faith was almost impossible to destroy because it was impossible to establish.

I had to get home and rest up. Body finding takes a lot out of me. I had an appointment with Kate Barnum. She didn't know that. Suddenly, we had lots to discuss. She didn't know that either. It was okay for her not to know these things. Today I'd learned there were plenty of things she didn't want me to know.

Soup's Done!

She opened the door to me. The mop of shaggy ringlets atop her head was captured in a stolen motel towel turban. I wondered just how big her collection of those towels might be. She pulled a cigarette out from between her unpainted lips and flicked it past me into the virgin snow. Dugan's Dump was quiet enough to let me hear its dying hiss. She bent to kiss me. I let her. I kissed her back, sort of. I kissed her the kind of kiss that raised questions. She was smart enough not to ask them. She knew about such kisses. She gave me a beer, told me to sit and excused herself. I waited.

She reappeared armed with a brimming bourbon tumbler, her turban-free curls dangling wet and disordered about pale cheeks. The white tails of a men's dress shirt hung far below the waist of her panties. A fresh cigarette had replaced the one that lay extinguished in the snow. The lips that held it were newly red and the air smelled of raw patchouli. She did not sit. I stood up.

"How's the research coming at the *Times?*" I accused more than asked.

"So far," she shrugged without much conviction, "it's a dead-"

I slapped her jaw with the back of my right hand. The tumbler and cigarette flew off to her left. The spinning cigarette's tip traced a red trail of its flight. Amazingly, most of the bourbon managed to ride out the launch intact, in glass. Contacting the stone fireplace ended that good fortune.

I'd like to say it was a playful poke and that she laughed it off with an endearing wink. I'd like to say that I was immediately overwhelmed with remorse and that even the thought of striking her again made me sick to my stomach. The fact was I smacked her down hard and it felt, if not tingly good, then, at least, satisfying.

She was down and before she could think of collecting herself, I was over her shoving stolen sheets of microfilm in her stunned face. "Dead end, huh?" I pulled her up by the shirt collar much as MacClough had done to me and held her face very close to mine. A red stain that wasn't smeared lipstick dribbled from the right corner of her mouth. I thumbed her chin clean.

"If it isn't Sir Walter Raleigh," she delivered straight-faced and then proceeded to spit in my eyes. I let her go and wiped.

"Why the lies, Barnum?" I didn't wait for an answer. "You were tryin' to cut me out of it. You were gonna go to print and leave me holdin' my dick in my hand. But we got a deal and you're sticking to it."

"Or else you're going to slap me again, Sir Walter?" she taunted, licking some fresh blood from her cracked lips. "Promises, promises."

"How long you have the articles about the trial?"

"A week, maybe. Ten days, maybe," the reporter turned her back on me to search for a new cigarette. "Long enough to figure out the Gandolfos pushed the button on Azrael Esther Wise. There!" she found the smokes.

"Well, if you got it all figured and you don't need me, where's your by-line, where's the revelations?" I picked up a copy of the *Whaler,* ripping it into ragged confetti. "Where, baby? Where?"

Barnum lit up the Chesterfield, blowing smoke as she spoke: "I'll print it when it's ready to print. Didn't your momma tell you never to serve the soup until it was all cooked?"

"We never discussed soup much, Mom and I." I tried smiling and failed.

"What are you all torn up about anyway?" Empowered by the cigarette, she went searching for more bourbon. "I practically had to drag you into this mess kicking and screaming. Now that I'm giving you the out, you don't want it. What's the buzz? I think we both know your buddy MacClough didn't whack the girl. And the stiff out back," she threw a thumb in the general direction of the pinky-ringed sapling, "he probably did the job and then got fed some of his own medicine. Silence is golden."

She was making sense, but it was sophistry. Her reasoning wasn't logic at all. It mocked it. If her story appeared now, MacClough would come out basically unscathed. And that's what I had gotten mixed up in this for. But if it came out now, no matter how much of a scoop it might be, the story's impact would be negligible and certainly not enough to resurrect a ruined career. We're talking about the murder of a forgotten witness from a forgotten trial. A murder committed by a forgotten man. No, she wasn't serving the soup because it wasn't done cooking.

"Nice try, Barnum," I applauded as if she'd sunk a thirty-foot putt.

That raised an eyebrow, but it didn't stop her from raising a new jigger of bourbon. "Cheers!"

"You're waitin' for Johnny's revenge," I slapped the bourbon out of her hand.

"Stop it," she screamed and swung at me wildly. I grabbed her wrists.

"You're biding your time for Johnny's revenge," I repeated.

"You're hurting me," Barnum twisted her arms like epileptic snakes.

"The story as it stands now won't do a thing for your career." I let go of the snakes. She stood back and rubbed their sore necks. "But let's say there's this Mafia kingpin;

dapper, stunningly handsome, a hero to some and current darling of the media. And let's say he gets whacked. While every other journalist this side of the Pacific rim is scratchin' their balls tryin' to come up with a 'Mafia War' angle, you serve them a love triangle and John Francis MacClough on a silver platter. Soup's done! Come and get it."

"You're talking crazy," she looked everywhere but into my eyes.

"Am I? Am I really?" I thought about making empty threats. I thought about throwing her husband's suspicious suicide in her face. I thought a lot of things and did none of them. "Okay, Barnum. We've got a deal. You're letting me out of it. I don't want out. You're gonna get your story and maybe we can pump it up enough to get you back to the top of the hill, but you're not climbin' up using Johnny's bones. There isn't gonna be any revenge killing. Got it?"

She did not reply. It really hadn't been a question.

"There's angles to this mess even you don't know about." I was thinking about O'Toole and Larry Feld.

"What angle? The dead cop?" she laughed at me, blowing smoke into my face. "I know about the dead cop. O'Toole, right? You're like a magnet for dead bodies." Barnum echoed Mickelson's sentiments.

"Other angles," I sounded unconvincing.

"Which angles might those be?"

"The bottom line is, without Gandolfo's demise you've got a story that will get you as far as your piece on zoning laws." The smile ran away from her face. "And like I said, there isn't going to be any more killing. Fact is, I've got all the info from you I require and all you've done lately is lie. The way I see it, you need me more than I need you. Without a fresh angle, you're dead in the water. You'll be penning zoning law articles for the rest of your fucking life. But a deal's a deal," God, I could be such a prince, "so you'll still get your story if there's one to be had."

"Oh, thank you," she got down on her knees and gave a mocking bow. "Oh, thank you my saviour," she stood. "Now get the fuck outta my house."

I got out. I was wearing my high school football coat and would until the Suffolk cops finished with my leather jacket. I remembered ordering the coat and the coaches telling me to buy it two or three sizes bigger than I was. I'd grow into it. I never did. Grow into it, I mean. But that was all right. Life buys us lots of coats we never grow into.

Humpty Dylan

Now I was guilty, plenty guilty. But that was about right. Fifteen minutes of denial is all I'm good for. There was no sense to slapping Barnum. Even the flash of satisfaction I'd felt in doing it had deserted me. All I had left was forever to beat myself up over hitting her. Yet neither that giddy prospect nor the guilt brought any relief.

My bones were cold from the inside out and my head was fat with pain. At least my ribs weren't barking. I took a handful of aspirins and jiggled them in my fist like craps table dice, then swallowed them with a gulp of bathtub water and submerged my head beneath the remainder. But even there, under the insulating water, something sang into my ears. In my tub the mermaids sang to me. Their lips moved, but I could not read them. The tune was familiar, but escaped me. I knew their song held all the answers, but I could not understand.

The phone snapped me out of my bathtub dreaming. I did not answer. I was in no mood to speak to another human and chose rather to listen for the siren's sweetly singing. But Bell's invention had broken the siren's spell and the answers I could not comprehend now teased me, ate at me like an object just out of reach or a name you know but cannot recall. The mermaid's song was becoming as annoying as an unscratchable itch.

The phone rang again. I was still in no mood for polite conversation, but I hoped answering the call might relieve my itch. So I dragged myself up from the depths and made my way to the phone, leaving sloppy wet footprints in my wake like the Creature from the Black Lagoon.

Nothing but a dial tone greeted me. Maybe the caller had simply tired of waiting for my gills and flippers to get to the phone. I'd like to think it was the mermaids trying to snap me out of my daze. In any case, going to the phone had helped. For now I recognized the specter that was taunting me. It was a question. If the Gandolfos *had* tracked and whacked Azrael and Johnny knew that, why hadn't MacClough taken his revenge? It just didn't jive. What was holding him back?

I returned to the bath; the pain in my head a little thinner, my bones slightly warmer and my guilt temporarily put on hold. But just knowing the question wasn't good enough. It never is, really. The time for answers was coming. I resolved to make it so. Aren't resolutions silly things? Sure, occasionally they're kept, but usually they fade with a night's good sleep.

My resolve, like the snow, had lasted the night. Unfortunately, so had my headache. I chugged down some more aspirin. I chose coffee to transport them. Coffee tasted better than bathtub water. At least mine did. You could not say the same for MacClough's. MacClough's coffee tended to taste like untreated sewage or the water at Coney Island beach. But that comparison is grossly unfair to untreated sewage.

I dialed Larry Feld's office and got his secretary, Madame Sunshine on the phone. She seemed almost as happy to speak to me as having a lung removed. I was just as pleased to speak with her. She put me through to Larry without the standard ten-minute waiting period.

"Klein?"

"Yeah, Larry," I confessed. "I got—"

"I got for you, too," he cut me off. "Did you know that reporter you had me check up on was pretty close to getting indicted for—"

"—murder," it was my turn to cut in. "Yeah, I heard something to that effect."

"You did?" Lean Larry sounded disappointed. "And I suppose you know about the Pulizer thing."

"None of the fine points, really. I stumbled onto this stuff after I asked you about it," I sounded apologetic. "But I need the details the way *you* get details."

"Details?"he sounded better. "I got details."

"Good. We can go over 'em tomorrow when I come to your office for our meeting."

"What meeting's that, Dylan?" Feld was too smart to overreact.

"The meeting between you and me and Dante Gandolfo," I tried my hand at nonchalance.

"Oh, that meeting. Let me check my calendar." Larry Feld was such a cool son of a bitch. I could almost hear his brain working out all the permutations. He refused to sound shocked or angry or surprised. "I don't see that down here, Dylan. Refresh my memory."

"Don't sweat it, Larry. Let's just say tomorrow about noon. Yeah, I like that. Noon."

"And what makes you think my client would be inclined to attend such a gathering," a faint edge finally appeared on the lawyer's voice.

"Just give him this message," drops of perspiration rolled along my sides and gathered on my brow. "Tell him, Azrael is in town and I know how to find her." I could hardly hear my words for the pounding of my heart.

"Who is—"

"Don't worry about who she is, Larry. Gandolfo will know."

"Do you know who you're fucking with, Dylan?" I could almost make out a bit of concern in his voice.

"I know, Larry. I know."

"I hope so. If this blows up in your face, I won't be able to put Humpty Dylan back together again."

"Just give him the message. 'Bye."

That really had been concern I heard in Larry's voice, but I wasn't fooled. Not after a lifetime of knowing Cassius. The concern was for himself, only himself and not for me. Larry didn't like being in the dark and that's squarely where I'd left him. That made him nervous. Little else did. Gandolfo would have lots of questions and Larry wouldn't have the answers. If he wanted answers he'd have to come to me. That was the idea. Unfortunately, I was only a little less in the dark than Larry.

Skull and Bones

The city drive was a lonely drive in winter. Farm stands, so alive in summer with berries and corn and gingham girls, were just hollow shacks now; flimsy and bent under the snow. The LIE was strangely hushed. Taillights and fenders of storm-abandoned cars peeked out at me from plowed drifts and icy shoulders. Greedy tow trucks, fat with the bad-weather bounty, flashed yellow lights my way as if saying: "You're next. You're next." Maybe they were right. Maybe I would be next. I don't know. In any case, that decision would not be mine.

When I walked into Larry's suite, ten minutes early, nearly drained of resolve and severely in need of a piss, he practically tackled me. Over his shoulder, I could see Feld's usually sour secretary smiling broadly. Larry busily babbled something to me in a panicky whisper, but I did not hear. I was too transfixed by the woman's smile. It said more things to me than Larry's words. It said she was pleased to see her boss so unnerved. That figured. Her smile also seemed to say: "You're next."

"I hope you know what the fuck you're doing," he cupped my face in his palm and aimed my eyes at his.

"I've gotta piss, Larry."

"Over there," the lawyer pointed absentmindedly to his right and repeated, "I hope you know what you're doing."

"So do I," I whispered.

"What?"

"Nothing, Larry. Nothing."

Larry retreated to his office, walking like a rattling bag of bones in a fancy suit.

I looked at sardonic Mary, the suddenly smiling secretary. She'd heard my whisper well enough.

"Do please hurry, Mr. Klein. We don't want to keep the gentleman waiting."

I ignored her and escaped into a world of azure tiles, porcelain fixtures sleeker than sports cars and framed prints of petunias in purple and black. I stood over the toilet, bladder exploding, unable to urinate. What was there to be nervous about? I'd done tougher things than confronting New York's most powerful crime boss. Sure, I'd done tougher things. But oddly enough, I couldn't recall any. Now I was sick to my stomach *and* unable to piss. Nice combination, huh?

Stepping out of the men's room, I noticed Mary had gone from her desk. Too bad, for I'd decided to puke on her lap if she were still smiling when I came out. So much for my plans.

I pushed Feld's door open without knocking. No one ran or jumped me or went for a gun. There were three of them, counting Larry. One, a man I took to be Gandolfo's bodyguard, stood between me and the other two men. He bettered me by half a foot and his shoulders weren't quite broad enough to land an F-14 on. He had a waist like Holly Golightly, legs like bridge supports and a neck with the diameter of a frisbee. He had a machine-made tan, jet black hair tied in a pony tail and wore an expensive suit purposefully loose. He was too pretty to be any good at bodyguarding. His type worries too much about his own goods getting damaged. Gandolfo probably kept him around for show or company or to drive his flashy cars.

Dante Gandolfo sat in Larry's chair, black leather boots on Larry's desk. Those boots cost more than what I was wearing from head to toe. Those boots cost more than my entire wardrobe. I wondered if he'd trade them for my football coat. I didn't put my wonder into words. The "Don" was even more handsome in three dimensions than in his pictures or on TV. But his black eyes, drained of fire and youth, detracted from his full lips, rugged lines and considerable dimple. His suit was a shiny gray, double-breasted Italian affair with a baby red rose pinned to properly wide lapels. His tieless shirt was black silk and he believed in using all of its buttons. In other words, he looked every inch the part.

Larry stood erect against a bookcase, practicing invisibility.

I opened my mouth to speak, but Gandolfo waved me off, closed his eyes in disapproval and shook his head no. I followed his advice.

"Vinny," he spoke at the pony-tailed muscle head, "why don't you wait outside for a few minutes?" It wasn't a question.

"But bosth," Vinny spoke with a nasal lisp, never taking his eyes off me, "I don't know about thith guy."

I raised my arms, opening wide my unbuttoned coat. It was a sign of submission, a sign that indicated I was willing to be frisked.

"That won't be necessary, Mr. Klein," Gandolfo graced me with speech. "Larry vouched for you. Put your arms down."

I put them down.

"Vinny," Don Juan returned to his original target, "go outside and keep Mary occupied for awhile. Take her to lunch. Better yet, take her to a motel. Must be ten years since she's had any."

"That old bitch!" Frisbee neck turned to his master for the first time since I'd walked in the room. "Sorry bosth, I'm picky about my fish."

"Then here!" Gandolfo exploded up from his seat and threw a fistful of pocket change at his boy. "Go to a fuckin' payphone and dial 1-900-Suck My Dick. Just get the fuck outta here!"

Vinny left without the scattered change or a word of protest.

"You," Dante Gandolfo, still risen and with a raised voice, turned to the invisible man, "wait for me outside."

"As your lawyer," Larry started to object, "I must respectfully advise that I remain—"

"You can respectfully kiss my ass. Now get the fuck outta here."

Larry departed, but I could see revenge in his eyes as he brushed past me. I remembered that look from childhood. It was a dangerous look. People always paid dearly for that look. The trouble was in deciphering for whom that revenge was intended: Gandolfo, for treating Larry like slave meat in his own office in front of me or for me, because I was the catalyst for the meeting? Worrying about Larry's vengeance was second on my list at the moment.

"Sit down, Mr. Klein," Gandolfo ordered me, sans histrionics, into a huge, bright red leather chair across from Larry's desk. "What do you know about me?" he questioned once I'd settled into the red beast.

"I read the papers. I watch TV. I hear things. So I guess I know as much or as little as any schmuck out on the street."

"Not just any schmuck, Mr. Klein," Don Juan bowed his head. "Not just any schmuck would know about Azrael or be ballsy enough to drag me down here like this."

"I'll take that as a compliment," I smiled, but nerves made it crumble.

"You take it however you take it," Gandolfo wasn't going to make this easy. "You want some coffee? I want some." He picked up the phone and pushed two numbers: "Hey Vinny, bring us some coffees." He covered the mouthpiece with his palm. "How you like yours?"

"Milk, no sugar."

Gandolfo frowned. "God, how do you drink it like that? But I suppose you take it however you take it," his full lips broke into a broad smile over his repetition of those words. He removed his hand from the phone: "Listen Einstein, one coffee, milk, no sugar and one triple espresso, four sugars," he paused. "That's right, genius, the usual."

"Thanks."

"Did you know I was a Yale man?" He showed me his perfect teeth.

"No." I figured one-word—one syllable, if possible—answers were best until I found out how he was playing this.

"Yeah, really. But Skull and Bones wouldn't have me. I suppose they thought I was already a member of a more powerful club. You see a man in my position has it tough. People fear me, but I get no respect. People are always confusing those two things; fear and respect. It's a chronic problem, but *c'est la guerre!*"

"That's war!" I translated.

"Good, Mr. Klein. That's very good," the Don applauded. "I'm telling you these things to help you understand."

"Understand?"

"Yes, to help you understand that I expect you to honor and respect what I'm about to say. I don't need you to fear me. You already fear me, but fear has its limitations. Fear didn't stop you from pulling this stunt. So I want you to pay close attention."

"Say your piece."

"I don't give a rat's ass about that Judas cunt, Azrael. Are you listening?"

"Very carefully."

"I don't care whether she's dead or alive and living in your back pocket or in Paris with Jacques Brel," he was shouting now, wiping sweat from his forehead with the sleeve of his suit.

The Mafioso doth protest too much. I thought it. I didn't say it.

"But this can't always have been your attitude about her," I tried playing shrink for a bit. "I heard you two were in love once."

"Sure, at first my father was out for blood," he confessed in an almost placid voice. "She tried to hurt me and my family. But that was a lifetime ago. I can't even remember what she looked like."

"Here," I produced the white-bordered Polaroid of Gandolfo and Azrael taken two decades ago, "maybe this'll help job your memory."

"Where'd you get this?" His tone was cool, detached, but his face had gone white.

"Let's just say I inherited it. Keep it."

"I told you to listen carefully," he was up, around the desk, standing over me. "Apparently, you didn't hear me," Gandolfo crumpled the photo like last week's grocery list and threw it in my lap. "I don't care if you know where she is. If you thought you were gonna get any money outta me or my people, you were wrong. Grandstand plays like yours only work in the movies. Didn't your mother ever tell you that believing in the movies can be detrimental to your health?"

"No and we never discussed cooking soup either."

"Huh?"

"Forget it." I waved carelessly at nothing in particular.

"I suggest you do the same. Forget why you dragged me down here and forget that we ever met. Forget—"

"Coffees, bosth," the lisping Adonis barged in.

"Mr. Klein won't be staying for his, Vinny."

I stood to go. I was being dismissed. Vinny remained frozen, coffee in hand, just inside the door. He gave new meaning to the term "dumb waiter."

As I got just past Vinny, Gandolfo called for me. I turned around.

"I know who you are, Mr. Klein. I know about you and that cop, that no good donkey prick, MacClough. I hope you're not here doing his bidding."

"Johnny doesn't know I'm here," I couldn't hold down my contempt. "He'd probably kick my ass if he did."

"That's good. I'd hate to think that potato-eating

motherfucker sent you here to stir things up, to cause a little anarchy," Gandolfo rubbed his hair with his palms. "I had a professor that used to say it was easier to shout anarchy than to create it. Do we understand one another, Mr. Klein?"

"We do." I closed the door behind me.

Outside the door I smoothed the crumpled snapshot and put it back in my pocket. Mary was back at her desk typing; her face had resumed its normal gargoyle pose. Larry stepped toward me but I shooed him away and headed for the bathroom. Pissing, like love, is better the second time around. Before I could get most of me out of the bathroom, Larry descended. He locked my left arm in his bony right and guided me into an adjoining office.

I took it to be a conference room. There were twelve mahogany and camel leather chairs with a matching table slightly shorter than most par fives, more audio and video equipment than at a third world television station, a small bar, a refrigerator and a cappuccino machine. It was sort of a yuppie version of heaven. Larry key-locked the door and slunk to the far end of the room like a cat prancing on bayonets. I just sat down. My bullshit threshold had long since been passed.

Larry produced a fairly stuffed envelope from the inside pocket of his suit jacket, sneered at it, squeezed it like a cantalope and slid it down the table at me.

"You'll make a hell of a shuffleboard player," I picked up the package. "What is it?"

"An en—"

"This isn't a sitcom, Larry, so spare me the straight lines. What's in the envelope?"

"Gelt, cash money," he yawned as he was wont to do.

"I'm a writer not a dentist. Don't make me pull teeth. Who from and who for?"

"He says you'll understand. You'll know who it's for."

"Gandolfo says?" I twisted my eyebrows into a question mark.

"Gandolfo says," lean Larry confirmed. "Open it up."

I did. The thousand dollar bills were so crisp and fresh that it was nearly impossible to separate them.

"There's one hundred of 'em," the lawyer offered matter-of-factly. "I've been instructed to inform you that five of those bills are yours as a tip for delivering the remainder to the proper party and that any debts owed by you to me have been taken care of, wiped clean."

"Nice tip," I palmed five bills off the top and put the rest back in the envelope. "Problem is, I'm still a little unclear who the cash is for."

"I've not been given any details on that matter," Feld spoke to me in his courtroom voice.

"But if you had to make a guess . . ." I trailed off.

"I'm not a guessing man, Dylan."

"But if you were?"

"I'd say there are some women some men never get over no matter how much hurt passes between them."

"Gandolfo just got done calling her a cunt and now you're telling me he wants me to fork over ninety-five G's to her."

"Mr. Gandolfo is a very complex man, Dylan," Larry's courtroom manner returned. "Sometimes it is in his best interests to say certain things and have me say others. I'm certain you understand." Feld looked at his Piaget like a buffoonish actor.

"I get the feeling class is out," I caught his drift.

"Yes, well . . . I do have other appointments. Oh, I almost forgot," the lawyer snapped his fingers, "Mary has a file for you. It contains that information on the Barnum woman. Interesting stuff. She was pretty close to needing my services. You'll see. And please be careful with it. The file contains, shall we say, certain documents that should have been impossible to obtain."

"I understand," I put my right hand out for Larry to shake. "I owe you one."

"No, Dylan. You don't owe me a thing," he shook my hand more firmly than I can ever remember his doing previously.

"One more thing, Larry. What if the envelope turns out to be undeliverable?"

"Apparently, you don't understand," Cassius screwed his face up. "There's no options here. You deliver that envelope one way or another. Good-bye, Dylan."

The typing gargoyle barely noted my presence when handing me the Barnum file. I didn't inspect the package but rather just stood there a moment observing the sour woman at work.

"Will there be anything else, Mr. Klein?" she asked, still refusing to look up. Actually it was more a dismissal than a question.

"Yes, Mary, there is. Why do you hate me?" A hundred thou in cash in your pocket makes such queries seem perfectly natural.

She ceased typing and looked directly in my eyes. "Hate is such an ugly word. I prefer contempt. That's better. Yes, much better. It's appropriately legalistic." She was almost gleeful.

"Contempt, then."

"Because you've known him your whole life," she pointed at an enlargement of the cover of the Post showing Larry triumphantly holding forth on some courtroom steps. Above his picture the headline read: 'Babysitter Strangler Slapped On Wrist.' "You know what he is."

"Better than most," I confessed to the truth.

"Then you have your answer," she stated as if she were Moses delivering the commandments.

"What about you, Mary?"

"Even whores judge people, Mr. Klein," she winked. "But don't fret, I have enough contempt for the two of us."

"He pays you well. I imagine you need the money. I need the kind of information he's good at getting. What's wrong with needing?" I wondered weakly.

"Sometimes, need's not a good enough excuse," the secretary shook her head sadly. "Besides, we don't really need him. His clients, they need him. We choose him, Mr. Klein."

I walked to the elevator, envelope in pocket, file in hand. I didn't argue with Mary. What good is it to argue with the truth?

Hickory Cure

Vinny, Don Juan's bodyguard cum coffee boy, was waiting impatiently by the lift doors, pressing the buttons like a hungry rat in Skinner's lab, looking to the arrows for a cue. My brain was too busy treading water to care much. I noticed him and I didn't. If he noticed me, Vinny didn't show it. Labs rats are like that. I decided the walk down would do me good.

When did I ever know what was good for me? The steps made my knees sore and my sore knees reminded me that healing ribs prefer elevators. Hell, my aches and pains were the up side of my descent of Everest. There are protozoa streetwise enough not to carry a tenth of a million bucks down deserted stairwells. Hello! I could've been rolled easier than a bagel and my body wouldn't've been discovered until the next fire drill.

So, I wasn't thinking straight. I was too preoccupied by today's episode of the Dante and Larry Show to think straight. Those two had blown enough smoke up my ass to hickory cure my colon. If Gandolfo truly didn't care about Azrael, why bother to meet me at all? Not coming would have made the point with more elegance than threats and denials. And if he did care, again, why meet me? Why give me an audience of lies and then turn me over to Larry for the big payoff? Why not let Larry do the bidding from the get-go? Why dress it up with whistles and bells and cheap theatrics?

I figured there were three viable explanations for the song and dance, all of them as appealing as a ruptured spleen. The

147

first possibility was Don Juan's being truly ignorant of Azrael's demise; that, as far as the Gandolfo crime family was concerned, Azrael Esther Wise was a bad memory still living under the auspices of the Witness Protection Program. But logic and the manner of her execution made that a difficult pill to swallow. The next possibility also depended upon the Gandolfos' being ignorant of Azrael's circumstances. In this scenario, however, the Gandolfos are still very interested in Azrael's whereabouts. Using me as a delivery boy, they flush her out of hiding to settle an old score. I found this one particularly unappealing since they'd have to get rid of me, too. The final possibility didn't hinge upon the Gandolfos' ignorance or good graces. In this version Dante knows Azrael is dead, but he's trying to protect himself by playing dumb and concocting an elaborate charade. It sounded nice, but it was too big a reach. Dante hadn't killed Azrael himself and besides the triggerman was busy turning into fertilizer under Dugan's Dump. And hey, a hundred grand is a pretty expensive charade even for a Gandolfo. Like I said, none of them seemed very credible explanations. Maybe there were other possibilities I just wasn't seeing. It wouldn't be the first time.

I sat on a bench in the metal and glass courtyard of Larry Feld's office building. Some people ate their lunches, some read the *Wall Street Journal*. Some couples kissed in dark corners. I drummed my fingers on the Barnum file and stared at the crinkled photo of Azrael with Don Juan.

"Who were you, really, Azrael?" I asked the girl in the snap, the girl from two decades past, not the made-up mannequin I had found by the tracks. "What was it about you? What *is* it about you that controls men from the grave?" I wanted to know. I was one of those men.

She did not respond. Maybe that was her secret; silence.

I had come for answers and came away with more questions. Maybe there were no answers. And that frightened me, maybe more than anything.

The Phoenix Myth

The Scupper lights fairly glowed in the blowing snow of blue dusk. MacClough stood behind the bar trying to flip quarters into a shot glass. Bob Street, proprietor of the Star Spangled Deli, and Stan Long, operator of Sound Hill's lone service station, sat belly-up and side by side next to the beer pulls. Stan was in his usual four-Scotch foul mood and refused to take the always jovial Street's action on MacClough's quarter-tossing prowess.

"Fucking snow," Stan Long muttered as I walked up.

"Bad for business?" Bob Street wondered and winked hello to me.

"Nah," the scotch drinker barked. "Business is too damned good. Snow don't give a man time to relax. After I leave here, I'll be making tow calls till sunup tomorrow. Fucking snow."

"Life's like that," Johnny commiserated.

"Black and Tan." I ordered out loud, although MacClough had poured the stout and ale before I spoke. "Yeah, Stan, I just drove in from a meeting in the City," I looked Johnny in the eyes as I spoke. "Cars stuck all over the place."

"Meeting?" MacClough nibbled at the bait.

"Must've been important for you to drive all the way into New York," Bob Street added as if on cue.

"Very important," my gaze fixed MacClough in his tracks.

"Fucking snow," Long slammed his rocks glass on the

bar along with a likeness of Alexander Hamilton. "Tomorrow," he spit an ice cube on the floor and exited.

"I'll be over there," I told MacClough, pointing to a table under the impotent harpoons. "Safe home, Bob," I patted the deliman on the back.

I laid Barnum's file open across the unsteady table. It was actually two files bound together with rubber bands. One dealt exclusively with the Pulitzer fiasco; the other with her husband's alleged suicide. Larry was amazing. J. Edgar Hoover had nothing over Feld when it came to obtaining inside info. Between them, the files contained internal memos from the *New York Times,* confidential reports from the N.Y.P.D. and personal notes passed between Pulitzer committee members. And to make things more accessible, each file came with a word-processed brief explaining certain intricacies that a layman might neglect and/or misinterpret.

Although Larry had neatly separated both incidents into distinct files, the circumstances surrounding each ran together like fingerpaints in the rain. Barnum was a hot young talent at the *Times* and she had been doing an investigative series on how organized crime directly affected the price of almost anything purchased within New York City. There was a set of articles on mob/union activities, a set on the garment district, a set on the airports and trucking and a set on the construction industry, the banking industry and a high profile set on the Mafia's infiltration of government and the courts. There were copies of her work in the file. Like I said before, Kate Barnum had teeth and she knew how to use them. But beyond her style, what gave Kate an edge were her sources. She claimed, in memos to the editorial staff, to have the highest-level sources within the unions, the Mafia and even in the government. She'd spent a lot of time doing these pieces, too much time.

Mike Tallenger was an attractive man in a beatniky sort of way. He had a gray pony tail, a salt and pepper soul patch, long sideburns that resembled Italy on an atlas and empty blue eyes. He was a jazzman, a sax player, a manic-depressive and the late second husband of Kate Burnum. Larry had provided a publicity picture. Tallenger had been at Juilliard, Berkeley and Bellevue. He met Barnum at the latter while she was working up a piece about New York's treatment of the homeless. Kismet it wasn't, but they got hitched anyway.

Between the two files, I worked out a rough chronology of their lives together. The first two years of marriage had been relatively uneventful. Uneventful, that is, if you allow for Tallenger's two trips to private hospitals out on Long Island. No more Bellevues for Mike, not with Kate's corporate insurance. The big trouble came in year number three, the year Kate began researching the Mafia infiltration series.

I didn't have to infer or deduce or read between the lines. It was all here in police reports, shrinks' reports and Barnum's own letters of confession and resignation. The reporter had started to spend a copious amount of time away from home. Tallenger was becoming delusional and increasingly paranoid. He told his psychiatrist that his wife was having an affair and that she and her boyfriend were planning to kill him. He confronted her. Her time away increased as did the confrontations.

She moved out. She began drinking. She began dating other men. She told one of her new beaus she was having trouble sleeping. He got her a script to ease that problem. The pills worked for awhile. In the end, nothing worked. Tallenger tried making nice, wanted to reconcile. She nixed the idea. One night a cop from the Fifth Precinct called her at her desk and suggested they meet at Tallenger's.

Tallenger had done his last gig. He'd never have to play another wedding or bar mitzvah to make ends meet. His end was met. The unstable sax man had consumed enough sleeping pills to kill a standing-room-only crowd at Shea.

Cops didn't find a note, but they did trace the pills back to Barnum and the prescription her new beau had supplied. Odd thing was, Kate swore never to have given any of the drug to Tallenger. Another odd thing happened. Three days after they found the permanently sleepy Tallenger, the cops received a package in the mail. You guessed it. The package was from Barnum's late husband. In it they found a note repeating Tallenger's accusation that Kate was plotting to have him executed. In addition, the deceased jazz man charged that Kate Barnum had recently had meetings with several known felons; some suspected of contract killings. Tallenger also claimed that his estranged wife had been busy trying to take out a life insurance policy in his name. It was all very dramatic, very Hollywood, but the cops looked into it anyway. And when they did, things got curiouser and curiouser.

Kate Barnum admitted to the meetings with the known felons, but asserted she was researching a story. When pressed for the names of these felons, Barnum refused on the grounds that these people were confidential sources. And a few insurance companies had records of calls from a woman asking if their firms covered people with a history of mental illness; specifically, manic depression. Even Tallenger's doctors thought there might be something to his suspicions as people suffering from his condition tended not to be paranoid or delusional. The cops smelled a rat, but the D.A. liked the case. He was sort of partial to fat headlines and reelection. The Grand Jury was less impressed and didn't have to worry about reelection. They refused to indict.

The victory was a small and fleeting one. In spite of the *Times'* best efforts to keep the Barnum business hushed, some of the details reached the ears of Kate's confidential sources. Fearing she might be forced to roll over on them to save her own neck or might subpoena them to testify in open court to corroborate her story, Barnum's sources cut her off and dried up like the Great Salt Lake. Without their help, Kate's big series was deader than Kelsey's nuts. She completed the work anyway. Unfortunately, it was a considerable batch of lies pieced together by an alcoholic journalist who was under police scrutiny and whose husband had recently committed suicide. She neglected to clue her editor into that fact, and he ran with it. The whole paper ran with it, advertising the Barnum series on local TV, on the backs of buses and in the subway. Kate's blue-collar appeal, showing how the average Joe's wallet is picked by organized crime, struck a resounding chord with people who usually read the *News* or the *Post* or *Newsday*. It was a coup built on a house of cards. The coup and the cards tumbled when a fellow reporter, who knew someone who knew someone who knew someone who worked for a member of the Pulitzer Award Committee, patted her on the rump and informed Kate she was a veritable shoe-in for the prize.

Barnum's admission of guilt was a blow to the *Times*, but not as severe as the one the *Washington Post* had received under similar circumstances. At least Kate hadn't actually been given the award. The *Post* reporter had to return hers. Kate resigned, kissed her career *au revoir* and went into unsuccessful alcohol rehab. The paper printed excerpts from her letter of resignation and an apology to its readers.

God, she *had* fallen and all the way down. Now she longed to be a phoenix risen from the ashes. But Barnum was reinventing the phoenix myth, for if she was to fly again, not all the ashes would be her own.

"The cops get back in touch with you?" MacClough sat across from me just as I was slapping the rubberbands about the Barnum files.

"Not yet," I looked around and noticed we were alone.

"Meeting in the City, huh?" Johnny had taken the hook and bait.

"Big meeting," I yawned a burlesque yawn. "The biggest."

"About your writing?" What, you finally get some agent with bad enough taste to take you on?" the ex-detective was straining.

"Answers for answers, MacClough. That's the way it's gotta be," I stood to go.

He grabbed my free arm. "Answers for answers."

I sat back down. "Tell me about her."

"I was just out of—"

"Not about you," I cut him off, "about her."

"What about her?"

I thought for a second. "Her name."

"Azrael?"

"Yeah, who names their kid after the angel of death?"

"Her full name was Azrael Esther Wise. The Esther was for her mom."

"But we," I caught myself, "Jews name only after—"

"—the dead," he finished. "Yeah, her mom died giving birth to her. So her father's this nutty bastard and he hangs the albatross on her forever. Then when she was four or five her dad got his right in front of her." John made a pistol of his thumb and forefinger and placed the barrel against my chest. "Bing. Bing. Blew his fucking heart out his shoulder blade. Murdered for a buck and change. Too bad in a way."

"How's that?"

"Azrael started believing, believing in the name. Believed it until . . ."

"The Dain Curse. A book," I explained before Mac-Clough could inquire. "Just a book."

I wondered if Azrael had ever read it. Maybe living it had been enough.

"The meeting," MacClough clapped his glass of Bush-mills down to let me know my turn had come.

"Here," I tossed an envelope on the unsteady table. "Take a peek. It won't bite."

"There's a . . ." the barman began counting.

"A hundred grand, give or take five thousand."

"How'd'ya come by this?" Johnny snapped a thousand between his fingers.

"An old running mate of yours: Dante Gandolfo." Mac-Clough threw his whiskey in my face. "It's for Azrael," I went on, using my sleeve to rub the burning Irish out of my eyes."Pretty strange, considering she's dead. Pretty fucking strange since we both know who had her whacked. I guess maybe we don't know. I guess that's why it's taken you so long to hit back."

"Get out," he didn't shout it. He didn't have to.

"What happened to answer for answer?"

"Get out," MacClough threw the neat pile of bills at me, their newness keeping them together. "I told you to stay out of it. This is my business."

"Not just your business anymore," I waved the stack of cash at him. "Now it's my business, too."

I left before MacClough could repeat his desire for me to exit. But there was no exit anymore, really. Not for him. Not for me.

Punch the Clock

I sat at the keyboard staring at the odd arrangement of letters. My fingers didn't find any combination of keys particularly appealing. I thought writing might help clear my head, but that was a typically silly notion. I usually needed a clear head to write. I turned everything over and over again. From Christmas Eve forward, I turned. But instead of crystallizing or sorting out, the facts just twisted together like a bucket of worms.

Since I couldn't mentally unscramble the case, I decided to spread it out on the floor, literally. I laid out every sheet of the Barnum files, all the pilfered microfilm, the article and pictures I found behind the portrait of O'Toole's dead kid. I even spread the sticky cash out, bill by bill and end to end. I took sheets of paper and wrote out the names of everyone I'd come in contact with since Christmas Eve—one name per sheet—and scattered them on the floor. Mojo's name looked up at me and Vinny's and Larry's and Sato's and Tadamichi's. On other sheets I listed events and the approximate times of their occurrence, i.e. I meet Barnum/After midnight, Christmas Day.

The assembled material took up considerable floor space and painted me into a corner. I sat there for a second, eyes closed, trying to reach back, squeeze out any details my weary head might have omitted. Once satisfied that there was nothing left, I walked the room. I stopped by each part of the patchwork and considered its merit, its relevance, its relationship to other pieces. That done, I ripped the mosaic apart, shrinking it down, removing names of people that had no bearing on the case, throwing out events that were inconsequential or led nowhere. The puzzle got smaller. I still hated puzzles.

Nothing jumped out at me and bit me on the ass. There were no revelations to make me slap my thigh and shout: "Eureka!" But, there was definitely something. Facts and things no longer stuck together like that bucket of worms. No, things were clearer. Arranged like the letters on my keyboard, the details of recent times were distinct but meaningless; or rather, their meaning was limited. With a typewriter keyboard, if you could hit upon the proper combinations, there were words and, sometimes, art. With my patchwork puzzle there would be no art, only solutions. Unfortunately, as in my vain attempts at writing, no particular combination appealed to me.

I slept a haunted sleep. Like a man who'd worked too many hours at his job, my dreams would not permit me to punch the clock. Sleep was work. There was a blackness to the disconnected images that flashed in my head. They weren't dreams, per se. It was more like the album cover game we played in college. After tripping out on acid, we'd sit in a totally dark room. I mean totally dark. We'd even tape up the door space. One of us would pull out albums and spark a cigarette lighter just beneath its bottom edge. That brief spark would burn the vision in your head like a photographic negative. That's what the pictures in my sleep were like, photographic negatives.

When I woke up, the negatives were gone, but my dreams had educated me. Even before pissing, I ran to the paper mosaic laid out on my floor. The answer was there. I was sure of it. Of all the names, events, articles and pictures that filled my sleep, there was only one I could not account for, explain away or discard. The key was a blurry woman getting into a blurry car in an overexposed photo taken from too far away. I should have understood that when I found her along with the articles and other pictures behind the portrait of the late O'Toole's late son. She hadn't been hidden there coincidentally.

I plucked her snapshot up from the floor, but I couldn't determine anything more about her or her hazy universe than I had when we first met. She was the point on which this whole nightmare turned. I knew that, somehow. I just did. Precisely who she was and where she fit in this dark chain of being, I couldn't say. She was an answer given in a foreign tongue to a question posed in English. Regrettably, I didn't speak the language and none of the people who did, would or could translate. But I could guess. Sometimes, I was good at guessing. Just ask my ninth grade French teacher.

I had some other hunches, too, but now was not the moment to ponder. It was all a bit much for me in the morning without a piss and coffee. I cleaned up the patchwork puzzle decorating my floor, putting the pieces back in their proper folders, envelopes or pockets. My next appointment was in the kitchen with a coffee pot. That taken care of, I headed for relief. As I did my long-delayed business, I looked in the mirror, making plans to prove myself prophetic.

The phone let me know there was at least one someone out there with little or no interest in my pissing or future as a prophet. I let the phone do its chirping thing until my answering machine kicked in.

"Klein? Klein!" Detective Mickelson's angry voice shouted over my recorded greeting. "I know you're there. Pick this up!"

I was inclined to disobey, but sensed that in the long run it was preferable to try and fence with him now than to have him come get me later.

"Yeah, what is it? Who is it? What time zone we in?" I tried sounding deathbed ill and marathon tired.

"You sound like shit."

"Thanks." I didn't lie. After all, he had bought the sick act.

"Seems like a regular thing for us, me calling you to come pick up a piece of clothing we run a nitrate test on. Maybe I should've been a French cleaners," Buddha belly smiled through the phone.

"As long as the tests show negative, I can live with it."

"Problem is, the stiff's you find, can't. Live with it, I mean."

"That's a joke, right, Mickelson?" I wanted this conversation to end.

"You know where to find me and your scummy leather jacket. You won't find one without the other."

It was tough, but I let that straight line pass untouched. "When should I find you?"

"Now," he commanded.

"Not now. Maybe later."

"Leave out the maybe. I'll be waiting." Something clicked in my ear.

I went back to the bathroom, finished what I'd started and got some coffee. I even got to drink some of it. I had a morning full of phone calls ahead of me. The first one was to Kate Barnum. We hadn't spoken since the evening I used her chin for target practice and, in the interim, I'd had a chance to read up on her tumble from grace and her husband's suicide. I decided no small talk would be best.

"Can you get me in to see the coroner or the doctor that did the bird woman's autopsy?" I followed my own advice and skipped the niceties.

"And a fine good morning to you as well, Sir Walter. Have you been working on your jab?"

"Can you or can't you get me in?" I refused to spar.

"Why?" A fair question.

"I need it for the soup."

"If I had to, I could manage it," she yawned.

"Manage it. Tomorrow or the next day," I ordered.

"Anything else, Sir Walter?"

"Yeah. You gonna be in the office later?" I wondered.

"No. Why?" the reporter was reasonably suspicious.

"Because I'm gonna be in town later and I thought we might straighten a few things out. "

"Like my jaw? I don't think I want to see you yet, Dylan."

"Fine. 'Bye."

Actually, in spite of my one word of feigned disappointment, I was glad that Kate Barnum would be out at Dugan's Dump all day. I had some questions to ask her boss. They were the kinds of questions I couldn't ask with her there to listen. They were the kinds of questions that had to do with hunches.

To play another hunch, I fetched my phone book and looked up a Louisiana exchange. I started to punch in the numbers for Baptist and Saviour Hospital in Baton Rouge when something paralyzed my finger. The number. There was something about the number. I'd seen it written someplace else, written in another hand. I shot up like I'd just sat on a skunk. I ran over to my writing desk where all the photos and files and articles were. I pulled out a list of phone numbers. Some were old and smudged and in pencil. Some were more recent and written in pen. And two of the numbers matched numbers in my phone book; one for Baptist and Saviour, the other for the Dixieland Pig and Whistle in Biloxi, Mississippi.

What an idiot I'd been not to make the connection until now. The day I found O'Toole dead, I had looked right at the sheet of phone numbers. Nothing had clicked then. It clicked now. MacClough's late partner had been sniffing along the same trail as me. That much was clear. What I needed to know currently was if he had followed me down that trail or had I followed him. If the latter was true, I'd have to do some serious rethinking about Terrence O'Toole's part in all of this. I put my fingers to the phone buttons again. This time I finished punching.

"Patient Records, Marie Antoinette Gilbeau speakin'," I would have recognized that bright voice even if she had omitted her name.

"Hey, yo, Marie Antoinette."

"Officer Bosco?" she hesitated.

"Detective Bosco, but dat's good. I said ya had a good ear, didn't I?" I couldn't give her roses so a compliment was the best I could do.

"Did y'all ever catch dat—"

"S'why I'm callin'," I cut her off to add to the sense of urgency. "We are real close, Marie Antoinette. I got an important question for ya."

"Anytin', detective, jus' ask."

"Ya said ya got two calls besides mine about Carlene Carstead; one from a reporta and one from a cop."

"Dat's right as mud on de delta," she confirmed.

"Now try and go back, way before my call or de ones we just mentioned. As far as a year ago, did anyone else evuh make inquiries about Carlene Carstead by phone or in person?"

She didn't answer right away. I wasn't sure what that meant, but it added to my already high opinion of the queen of France.

"Sorry, Detective Bosco, but d'answer gotta be no," she sounded hurt.

"Hey, don't sweat it. I ap—"

"Ya know," Marie stepped on my words, "even folks workin' in dem hospitals been takin' sick days every now and den. Let me check wid de girl dat sits fa me when I'm out."

"It might speed stuff up some if I describe de suspect I'm wonderin' about."

Marie Antoinette agreed with that notion. I described O'Toole as best I could and said he might've claimed to have been a cop. She offered to call me back, but I told her the New York taxpayers wouldn't mind me waiting on hold. Besides, I didn't feel like explaining my Long Island area code to her.

"Shaw 'nough, detective, dat man been here. Priscilla Odile's positive. Big man wid a nose as red as boiled crawfish, even had a New York policeman's badge. Priscilla say she know dat from de television. She recalls him askin' 'bout dat little girl."

"Does she remember when?" a stream of sweat was running alone my spine.

"Dat would be 'round de terd week in August, lass year. I was down de bayou visitin' and Priscilla Odile had my desk dat whole week."

"I could kiss ya, Marie Antoinette." I could have.

"Well, if ya down Louisiana and ya don't . . ." she trailed off.

We spent a few minutes on the good-byes. I determined that if and when things got settled, I'd write her a letter explaining what had really gone on and who I really was. There are just some people on this earth that deserve to understand.

I understood now that O'Toole had flushed Azrael out of hiding. He had tracked her down. But why? It was hard for me to accept that he woke up one August day and decided he had nothing better to do. No, someone had come to him. But who? And why O'Toole? I was pretty sure it wasn't Dante Gandolfo. If he had wanted Azrael's hide, he'd have better resources than some broken-down drunk of a retired cop. The truth is, I was convinced Don Juan had no part in whacking his old flame. Oh, I didn't buy that bullshit about his not caring or knowing whether Azrael was amongst the dead or the living. But if it wasn't Gandolfo . . .

I made a call to the Dixieland Pig and Whistle, the place Azrael, alias Carlene Carstead, once managed. I originally had planned it as a call of discovery, but talking with Marie Antoinette had transformed it into a call of confirmation. The new manager was a nice fellow and he was a sucker for my Brooklynese and New York Detective schtick. They all were. I spoke to about ten employees before I found one who could remember another Yankee cop fishing around about Carlene. Sue Anne Maples, an assistant manager, told me that the Yankee cop had called a few times and once even spoke to Carlene herself. Carlene had been real upset by that call. About a week later, she took a leave of absence. They all wished me luck in finding Carlene's killer. I didn't bother explaining that Carlene Carstead had drowned a very long time ago.

Okay, someone approaches O'Toole to track down Azrael. He finds her in Biloxi, Mississippi. But instead of going to his employer, O'Toole talks to her on the phone, warns her she's been found. That's the first thing that doesn't make any sense. The second is that instead of going to her guardians at Witness Protection and letting them know she's been found out, she runs straight back to New York. It's tantamount to pouring antelope blood over your head and running into a lion's den after twenty years of hiding in the tall grass. What could O'Toole have said to her? What did he know? I thought about the blurry woman and wondered if O'Toole's call had been about her. I went and got her picture again.

I called the other numbers on the sheet. One was disconnected. One was for Delta Airlines reservations. One was a local liquor store. Gee, what a surprise. And one was either a bust or a revelation. I couldn't know that yet.

"Hello, I'm—"

"Uncle Jack," a little boy shouted in my ear. "Mommy, it's Uncle Jack." The excitement in the boy's voice told me Jack had a nephew who loved him.

"Sorry, son, but I'm not—"

"Hello, Jack," Mommy got on the phone. "Jack, are you in New York or calling from the office?" Mommy had a throaty, inviting voice with a bit of sadness around the edges.

I looked at the picture in my palm and decided to drag out Detective Bosco, N.Y.P.D., yet again. If it ain't broke, so the saying goes. But I would have to tone down the "dems and dose." New Yorkers can spot a fellow New

Yorker's theatrical Brooklyn accent faster than a pig finding fungus in a truffle truck.

"Sorry to disappoint you and your son, ma'am, but I'm
not Uncle Jack."

That was followed with a few seconds of confused
breathing and silence. When the woman at the other end
refused to pick up the baton, I introduced myself as Detective Bosco. Not of Missing Persons this time, but of Homicide.

"Homicide?" she repeated with equal parts of shock and
skepticism.

Beside the delicate dialect problem, skepticism was
something else I was likely to encounter with a New
Yorker. After only three syllables, I could tell this wasn't
going to go as smoothly as my calls below the Mason-
Dixon line. Hey, no knock on southerners. It's nice to
deal with people who don't consider trust passe. Growing
up in New York, you lose your diapers and then you lose
your capacity to trust. Maybe it has to do with how we're
toilet trained.

"You must be mistaken, Detective Bosco," she assured
me with grave certainty. Then the ramifications of who I
was pretending to be sank in. "God, nothing's happened
to my parents. God!" she was panicking. I could hear her
son in the background asking if everything was okay with
Uncle Jack. "It's not Uncle Jack, Max. Please, shut up for
a minute," she screamed at the poor kid. He was crying
now. I was feeling pretty low.

"No. No. Nothing's wrong with your parents," I tried
sounding as reassuring as a Hollywood priest. And, before
she could ask: "And as far as I know, everyone else in
your family is fine, Missus . . ." I wanted her to fill in the
blank.

"You don't know my name?" the panic was replaced by
a mixture of anger and good old skepticism. "How dare
you call me up and scare me like that? I want your badge

number. What kinda cop are you?" She went on that way
for a minute or two. I let her. I deserved it.

After she calmed down, I explained that her phone
number was included on a list the police had found at the
scene of a homicide and that it was my job to check all
the numbers out. She wanted to know who'd been murdered. I told her. She didn't know any Terrence O'Tooles
or Johnny MacCloughs. She had never heard the name
Azrael before, but liked it. She'd heard the name Gandolfo
before: "Doesn't he pitch for the Mets?"

I laughed. She laughed. She told me her name: Leyna
Morton. It was unfamiliar to me and I was certain she
didn't pitch for the Mets. I suggested that her husband
might have a connection to some of the people I'd mentioned. She thought it unlikely. In any case, they were
divorced and he didn't have access to her phone number.
It had been an ugly affair, their divorce; custody battle et
al.

My heart sank when I heard that. I'd found a painfully
logical reason for Leyna Morton's number to appear on a
sheet of paper in a dead cop's abode. It wasn't the reason
I'd been fishing for. So much for my hunches. Nostrada-
mus was safe. Obviously, Mrs. Morton's ex had hired
O'Toole to do a little divorce work. Divorce work is
pretty profitable and lots of cops do it on the sly. You see,
it's easy for cops, even retired ones, to acquire unlisted
phone numbers and addresses.

"Do you have work and home numbers for Mr. Morton?" I went through the motions of getting info on her
ex-husband. I'd call him and coerce him into admitting
he'd hired O'Toole. Detective Bosco strikes again!"

"His name's not Morton," my phone companion informed me. "It's Tanzer. Mine's not Morton either really,"
Leyna swallowed her words. "I'm a little punchy from the
divorce and I wanted to make certain you really were a
cop and not some guy my ex-husband hired to track me

down," it was irony worthy of Dickens. "My name's Leyna Brimmer."

"It's okay. I understand," I was the Hollywood priest again.

"It's funny," she said more to herself than to me.

"What is?"

"I don't really know my family name. I'm adopted," she sighed. "You try not to think about it, but—"

"Please hold," I put the receiver down, ran back to my files and did some quick arithmetic. "I'm gonna ask you a strange question, Miss Brimmer," I wasn't in the mood to get permission. "Were you born in March of nineteen sixty-seven."

"Good guess," she sounded wary, "but no cigar. April sixty-seven. Why do you ask?"

"Just a hunch."

So full of my own genius, I got off the phone without getting the husband's numbers. Unconsciously, I guess, I didn't want to speak with him. No. I didn't want to hear him contradict my theories. Because, if I was right, the blurry picture in my palm had just sharpened considerably. Some questions would be answered and others would simply disintegrate like cotton candy in your mouth. I might even be able to answer the question that had plagued Leyna Brimmer her whole life.

Their Own Shadows

I did a rarely sensible thing and paid a visit to my safe deposit box. In it I placed the pertinent documentation I'd gathered, stolen, or stumbled onto since the night before Christ's birthday. I also managed to squeeze in two other items; a few neatly word-processed sheets outlining what the hell I thought was going on and the bundle of one hundred large in its original envelope. In a giddy moment, I'd entertained thoughts of just depositing the big money directly into my account and giving the teller apoplexy. Even in these days of junk bonds, arbitrage and leveraged buyouts, a hundred thousand dollar cash deposit will raise eyebrows and blood pressures. And let's face it, Suffolk Midfork Trust ain't the Bank of England.

I stood out in the street and the snow for a minute, admiring the bank. The bold Victorian dated back to the dying reign of Conrad Dugan. This quirky conglomeration of clapboards, granite, gingerbread spindles, turrets and a widow's watch was to have been Dugan's great house. His empire failed before he'd slept a night inside. The bank took it. The bank kept it. It had been a bank, with one name or another, ever since. I wondered what Conrad Dugan would think of automatic teller machines in the pantry. I think he'd probably like them.

I turned my back on the bank and trudged down Main Street to the less than considerable offices of the *Sound Hill Whaler*. I'd been in bigger cab stands and in train station toilets that were cleaner and less cluttered. But the first amendment says something about the press being free, not clean. An acne-faced teen-age boy I took to be a high school intern sat at a computer terminal mesmerized by its orange light, picking unconsciously at his acne-ravaged nose. Whistina Knox, the *Whaler*'s waspy, matronly business manager, was on the phone arguing the merits of advertising in her publication as opposed to the local pennysaver. She didn't seem to be winning, but managed to smile at me politely and acknowledge my existence. I pointed to my left and mouthed the name, "Ben," to her. She smirked and waved me in.

Ben Vandermeer's family went back to a time when most Long Islanders wore feathers and buckskins and Jay Gatsby was still a few centuries away from moving to West Egg. Vandermeer's family had been old money, but thanks to Black Tuesday, only the old remained. Ben learned his craft at the *News,* the *Brooklyn Eagle* and the *Tribune.* Mailroom clerk to managing editor; he'd done it all. In the late sixties he bought the *Whaler* and has been its only editor ever since.

"Ben," I rapped my knuckles on the inside of his office door. He sat with his back to me, thin wisps of white hair limply hanging over the top of his chair.

"What?" he swiveled around. "Oh, it's you, Dylan. I thought it was that pimply-faced twit the high school saddled me with. Used to get good interns once."

"Kate Barnum, for instance?"

"For instance," he raised his Fuller Brush eyebrows. "You here to talk or collect my bar tab for MacClough?"

"The former."

"Talk, huh? Shut the door and sit." He waited for me to follow his instructions. "Katy Barnum," Ben began, sensing what I'd come about, "was the best damned intern that travesty they call a high school ever sent me. At seventeen, Katy could out-think and out-write most of the cigar-smoking old farts I'd run across at the city papers." He grabbed a dormant pipe out of an ashtray and put a lighter to its bowl. "But I don't suppose you came in here to discuss Katy as an intern," Vandermeer blew sweet smoke my way.

"Maybe another time."

I flipped my safe deposit box key into his ashtray. I slipped a signature card out of my pocket and asked him to fill in the blanks. He did so without question and slid the card back into my palm.

"I'll drop this off at the bank," I waved the signature card at him. "I promised Kate Barnum a story, but there's a chance I may not be around to keep my word. I think I'll be okay, but you never know. Even if I maintain my health and boyish good looks, there'll be some people pretty anxious to get their mitts on the stuff in that box. If anything should happen to me . . . You know the script. And if nothing happens, I want someone known only to me with access to the goods."

"Big story?" the old newspaperman tried to act nonchalant, but I knew he could almost taste it.

"Barnum thinks so."

"Why give me the key? Why not your Brooklyn soul mate or, better yet, Katy herself?"

"I've got reasons, Ben. Look, if you don't wanna get in-"

"The key'll be in my safe when you want it back. You just call me if you need any other help." He extended his hand and I shook it.

"Remember Christmas Eve, Ben?"

"I remember about sixty-five of them," Vandermeer choked on pipe smoke, giggling at his rare wit. "When you found Jane Doe on the platform? I remember."

"Was Kate assigned to work late that night?"

All the giggly merriment went out of Ben Vandermeer's face. Something had just occurred to him that had come to me in my night of black flashing dreams. He didn't need to answer. His face had already spoken.

"The *Whaler*'s closed on Christmas Eve and Christmas Day. It's tradition," he put lyrics to the sad music of his expression.

"Strange thing, Ben, your Katy just happening to be conveniently on the scene; pad, pen and mini-recorder in hand. *Newsday* carried it as a wire service story and didn't even have a reporter call me until the day after the holiday. Was she in town working on anything?"

"No reason for her to be around that I can think of. The *Whaler* isn't exactly on the cutting edge of investigative journalism," the pipe smoker tested a smile and failed it. "And what's in Sound Hill to investigate on Christmas Eve anyway?"

"Zoning variances?" I prodded.

"Any newspaperman knows the right questions to ask. Only the good ones know what questions not to ask. Dylan, I've always flattered myself by believing I fall into that second grouping," Ben put down the pipe and ran his age-spotted fingers through the sparse white clouds of his hair, "but I'm gonna ask you one I shouldn't just the same."

"So ask."

"How deep is Kathy involved?"

"I don't know yet," I took a breath big enough for two. "But if she's in up to her toes or the shit's above her eyeballs, it doesn't really matter. Does it Ben?"

"I thought that ugliness at the *Times* might've taught her something," the old reporter went limp with defeat. "Her career was shot and I was hoping she'd adjust to it back out here in the boonies. I was gonna turn the *Whaler* over to her someday."

"If you were an all-star backstop for the Mets and got thrown out of baseball for drugs or gambling, how would you adjust to being the bullpen catcher for Oneonta?"

"I never looked at it that way."

I nodded and started out of Ben Vandermeer's office, but his curious voice called me back.

"If she's dirty, Dylan, why give her the story?"

"Dirty or not, she's worked harder for it than you could ever know. In an odd way, Kate's earned it."

I never made it to the bank. Dusk had crept into town while my back was turned and all humanity had fled the confines of Suffolk Midfork Trust. The cash machines in Dugan's pantry had no use for signature cards and I no use for them. The safe deposit box routine was pulp novel kitsch, yet I'd seen it work to perfection.

On my way over to the Star Spangled Deli, more than the wind gave me a chill. The lights in the Scupper were flicking off and a few seconds later MacClough's paws appeared at the front door flipping over the "We're Open" sign. Eventually the busy hands vanished and the sign read, "Sorry, We're Closed." Johnny would leave through the alley. That was natural enough. Only problem was, normal closing time was seven hours away.

I thought about following him. Don't believe that TV shit about cops. Cops can't follow their own shadows without a roadmap and an itinerary. And they couldn't spot a tail if it was stuck to their asses. Johnny was better than most. I'd seen evidence of that myself, but he was still a cop; retired, but a cop just the same. Cops wear uniforms to stick out, to be a presence. They want to be seen. They strive to be seen. Even their unmarked cars stick out like armadillos at a dog show. And because they're so accustomed to being observed, they have trouble spotting individuals in the audience. It's a difficult mind-set to shake.

Insurance investigators, even rusty ones, are like road chameleons. But to shadow MacClough, I'd have to be a stealth fighter or just plain invisible. He knew my car and, given my refusal to back off, he might be looking over his shoulder for it. After a minute's meditation, I realized there was no need to follow. I knew where he was headed. His time to act had come. I ran back into Ben Vandermeer's office and commandeered his phone.

Mr. Wizard

I didn't know what I'd do when I got there, but I was going. I didn't know how I'd find MacClough when I arrived. Maybe I'd just wait for the sound of gunfire and follow its report. For months the tension coiled and now the spring was unwinding. As I raced foolishly along the snowbanked expressway, I wondered about the spark that had initiated the gyre's unraveling and who might be felled by its blind momentum. The answers lay an hour away, across the bridge in Staten Island.

At the Knapp Street exit of the Belt Parkway, my soul shifted moods and, for a few moments, I could ponder summers of stickball and fireworks at the beach. Knapp Street marked the far border of my old neighborhood and until my ancient Volkswagen passed Cropsey Avenue, my heart would refuse all thoughts of Mafia kings and fallen maidens. From the parkway you could see D trains crossing noisily overhead. Their metal wheels shooting stars at the night, grinding along the tracks to and from Brighton Beach. Just east of the subway trestle sat the concrete bunker that had been my junior high school. I often imagined Hitler taking more comfort there than any seventh grader.

Further on, where the road rises and falls over Ocean Parkway, you pass the white brick butcher shop called Coney Island Hospital. Then, just ahead, came Lincoln High School. I always looked in back of the school at the football field, for it was there that I'd known my only moments of glory. It's tough to stare forty in the face having left your glory in the grass and mud behind your

175

high school. Tonight my glory was entombed in a gray foot of Brooklyn snow. But the skeleton skyline of the Coney Island rides, rising above the horizon like the bones of dormant dinosaurs, pulled my heart up through the snow and into the present. I was passing Cropsey Avenue. Soon, I would see the bridge.

There, spreading out across the moonlit narrows between Brooklyn and Staten Island, was the Verrazzano, its cold, ashen paint negating the span's majesty. I could recall a time when only ferries held the two boroughs together and trips to New Jersey were partly a sea adventure. And when bridge construction began, two slab footings rose up from the water like tombstones. But the bridge's completion meant more than easy trips to Jersey, for with any bridge comes migration. Once the Staten Island Expressway was flanked by sad houses on lonely hills. Now town houses and shopping malls dominated the landscape. Why should Staten Island be any different from the rest of America?

The Verrazzano had other effects beyond the destruction of the Brooklyn ferry. White, blue collar families—mostly Italian, some Irish, a few Jews—with a stomach for the stink of Jersey, the perfume of landfill, and disregard for increased cancer risk, ran gladly across the span to a suburb in the city and away from the Great Society, overcrowded streets and the *melanzane*. In Italian, *melanzane* translates into dark skin. In slang, it translates into niggers. And like all migrating hoards, the blue collars brought along their parasites. A handful of Mafia dons, always out of place and out of touch on Long Island, found nirvana in Staten Island. From their gaudy castle compounds in the Todt Hill section of the borough, they could run the family business by the swimming pool and be just fifteen minutes and a toll away from their territories. I was headed for one of those castles right now, but I doubted if the Gandolfos were out back taking a swim.

I held the hastily scribbled directions against the steering wheel, alternating glances between word-map and road. Larry Feld hadn't been eager to turn over the address nor had he coughed up the directions easily. He also didn't appreciate my request that he not phone ahead to the Gandolfos. I understood his position. Although the whereabouts of the Gandolfo digs aren't a national secret, the family would not be pleased with Larry for giving out the info without permission. But they could get over that. However, if Larry neglected to warn his client of impending danger—which MacClough's behavior clearly represented—and some harm were to come to the Gandolfos, Larry was as good as dead. As Feld put it: "Those guys will make cutting my balls off seem like a suspended sentence."

Let it suffice to say that it took all I had to convince Larry it was in his best interest to acquiesce to my demands. It was an amazing conversation, but that's for some other time. After promising Larry that I'd never disclose who'd given me directions, I asked him if he knew what all this lunacy was about. He said he had a pretty good idea. I asked him if he knew a woman named Leyna Brimmer. He said he didn't. That question made him curious, but I held him at arm's length. I said good-bye. All he said was: "Watch out for the old man." I promised I would, though I wasn't at all sure what he meant.

At the moment I was busy watching out for landmarks and streetsigns. The roads were remarkably well plowed given the recent weather, but that's always the case in an area with a concentration of top level Mafioso. I'd never been through this neighborhood before, but I was willing to wager the mail got delivered early, the garbage got picked up quietly and on time and that around here the crime rate dipped into negative numbers. Wiseguys have always understood the value of intimidation and big tips. No one servicing these homes got five bucks and Grandma's fruitcake for Christmas.

I knew I was close to my final destination when I saw

it. The "it" I refer to is the former residence of the late
don Pauly "Ping Pong" Palermo. The Cemetery, as the
estate is affectionately called on the street and in the press,
was Don Palermo's monument to ill-gotten money and
bad taste. I had only heard about its pink-rock perimeter
wall and statue garden replete with a black marble repro-
duction of Stonehenge, a plaster animal menagerie and a
circular arrangement of eleven eight-foot-tall bathtub
Marys painted alternately in red, white and blue and
green, white and red. You could see where the place got
its nickname. The main building was sort of a combination Bates Motel, amusement park funhouse and mauso-
leum topped off by a satellite dish big enough to gather
residual radio waves from the Big Bang. The place was
such a disaster, even Don Palermo had trouble cajoling
and bribing the appropriate functionaries into letting him
build it as planned. In New York, where the unofficial city
motto is "I never met a bribe I wouldn't take," that speaks
volumes. When "Ping Pong" went ding-dong outside a
Brooklyn luncheonette, the cops said he was whacked by
a rival gang member. I think it was the editor of *Better
Homes and Gardens.*

   I left the Cemetery behind and rolled to a stop along
the curb about a block down the hill from where Larry
had said I'd find the Gandolfo stronghold. Mine was the
only car parked on the street for as far as I could see ahead
or behind me. I didn't like that. Nor did I like being downhill from the house. If I was forced to approach the place,
Gandolfo's soldiers would have a fair chance of spotting
me no matter which direction I came from. Never underestimate the value of taking the high ground. Clearly, the
Gandolfos didn't.

   Okay, so now I was here and no bands played Stars and
Stripes Forever and the borough president wasn't waiting
to greet me. Back in Sound Hill I thought I might work
out a plan by the time I got on location. The fact was, I
hadn't worked anything out and the only thing I could

think of were the gargantuan Virgin Marys huddled like
a football team in Pauly Palermo's yard.

I stepped out of my car. The rotten-egg breeze blowing
in from Jersey was strong, but not howling strong and the
only sound on the street was the creaking of the trees like
an old man's knees in the morning. When the gusts died
down, even the trees were silent. I hesitated to put my
feet in stride for fear of their signature echoing in the silence and the sulphur of the night.

I waited for the wind to come up again. When it did, I
walked further down the hill to the last intersection I'd
passed. There were a few curb-parked cars adorning the
cross street, but none of them was MacClough's '66 Thun-
derbird. I hadn't really expected to spot it on the boulevard. He'd probably parked it a neighborhood away and
taxied up here. Maybe he made the trek on foot. Maybe
he wasn't here at all. Yeah, and maybe we were all just
angels dancing on the head of a pin. Johnny was around.
I could feel it. I turned back to my car.

Five steps up the hill I thought I heard a footfall crushing
snow behind a high hedgerow which ran parallel to the
curb. I stood my ground and held my breath like some
teen-age cheerleader in a cheap slasher movie. I waited for
another step in the snow somewhere behind the bushes. I
could feel the sweat leaking down my back, my heart
thumping so hard it hurt. For a few seconds, nothing.
Then it came at me, the curved mirrors at the back of its
eyes reflecting the streetlight shine. I jumped, not quite to
Delaware. Fucking cats! At least hockey masked mutants
with razor sharp machetes don't purr and nuzzle your
ankles after springing from the indigenous vegetation.
They may well hack your limbs off, but they don't nuzzle
and purr.

When my calico companion had tired of laying scent
claim to my lower extremities, she sat, licked a paw or two,
and looked up. She was clearly puzzled by my nervous
laughter and presence there in the gutter in the midst of her

territory. I tried to convey that I was equally confused. The mood changed suddenly. Her head twitched left then right, eyes widened, now glowing with fresh light. She darted. A horn blew. Tires screeched. I jumped to the bushes.

"Fuckin' asshole!" the unseen driver shouted at me and pulled away.

Too bad he left in such a hurry. I wanted to compliment him on the accuracy of his assessment. I stood, brushing my scraped palms against each other as a toddler might when leaving the sandbox, and took a few shaky paces up the hill. When I reached a gap in the hedgerow, something cold, hard and round pressed into the back of my neck. Mr. Wizard once explained that steel isn't actually colder than other materials. It's cold to the touch because it absorbs heat from our flesh. Obviously, Mr. Wizard had never had the barrel of a gun pressed against his neck. Gun metal is very cold. Trust me on that.

Never mind Mr. Wizard. Some awfully ugly thoughts went rattling around my head. Larry had phoned ahead to cover his ass and I was going to be hung out to dry. Maybe not. Maybe one of Gandolfo's boys had spied me from up on the hill and had come down to check me out. Maybe this was another wiseguy's house and he didn't like me playing with his cat. In any case, I wasn't looking forward to the rest of my life.

"Just take an easy step back and join me. I'm kinda lonely behind here since ya scared the cat away," casually ordered the voice attached to the man attached to the pistol.

Usually, I have real problems dealing with authority, but I've found that placing a gun on my neck is an effective short-term therapy. This time though, the weapon was unnecessary. I followed the casual commands and came face to face with my therapist.

"Hey, MacClough," I smiled. He didn't.

"That guy in the car was right," the ex-detective greeted

me, holstering his stubby .38. "You *are* a fuckin' asshole. Why couldn't ya just stay out of my business?"

"Because it isn't business and it's not just yours. I was the one who let Azrael walk outta the Scupper that night. I was the one who found her body." That made the tough cop grimace. "No, Johnny, whatever this is, it isn't all yours."

"And what the fuck do you know about anything?"

"Stop it, MacClough," I admonished in a furious whisper.

"Stop what?" He was good at a lot of things. Acting innocent wasn't one of them.

"I know, Johnny. Maybe even more than you."

"Get outta here. I got work to do," my therapist gave me a symbolic shove on the shoulder and started to turn.

"I know about the baby."

He stopped turning. "The ba—"

"Yeah, MacClough, the baby. Azrael's daughter."

The night went silent again. The wind, regaining its throne, blew swirls of loose snow at the sky and into our human faces. Johnny closed his eyes, and tried to let the wind scrape away two decades worth of questions and pain. We both understood that the wind was doomed to fail.

"How did you find out?" he asked, interrupting the pain.

"Would you believe it came to me in a dream?" I wasn't lying.

MacClough formed a bitter smile with his closed lips and pushed spurts of moist air thru his nostrils.

"Is she yours, Johnny?"

"Could be his," MacClough pointed up the hill. "I don't know. What I do know is that she's Azrael's. That was always enough for me." He didn't really believe that, but this was neither the time nor place to debate the matter.

"How'd you find out about the baby?"

"About two years after the Gandolfo trial, I was in the federal courthouse in Manhattan to give testimony in a drug case. I'm walking outta the mens room and this FBI type bangs into me. He apologizes and whispers in my ear to look in my coat pocket when I get home."

"A note?"

"A letter."

I felt like asking all about it, but I could pretty much figure out its content. Anyway, my feet were getting cold and I had the feeling that my solitary Volkswagen was going to start attracting the wrong kind of attention.

"I don't suppose I can talk ya outta tryin' to get in there?" I lapsed into nervous Brooklynese.

"No. There's some things that've been waitin' over twenty years to get settled. I'm tired of waitin'."

"Then I'm comin' along for the ride." I smiled. He didn't.

"No."

"Listen, MacClough. I could waste some more time reasoning with you, but I'm tired and my brain's tired of being twisted in knots," I walked right up in his face. A very red flag thing to do to someone from Brooklyn. "The bottom line here is if I don't get in, you don't get in."

"Back off," he warned.

"I'm gonna march up to the *goombah's* front gate and announce very loudly your intentions. I figure someone might be interested. So you got an easy choice. Take me or shoot me."

The ex-detective rubbed a pensive hand along his chin and screwed his face up with thought. "Okay, ya crazy fuckin' Jew," he said reaching one hand behind his back and reintroduced his .38," have it your way." Johnny held the gun's stub nose so close to my eyes, I could practically see its rifling. He smiled. I didn't.

"You're not gonna shoot me," I scoffed with all the self-assurance of blind tightrope walker wearing spiked heels.

"One shot and those boys on the hill will be down here like Italian lightening."

He put the gun down, laughing: "I surrender. I surrender. You wanna get killed, fine. Better they do it than me."

"My, what a comforting thought."

"Here's the deal," MacClough instructed. "They got good security up there, but even the best security gets lazy. No one's tried to whack a Gandolfo in years. The biggest threat those greaseballs usually face is from some smart-ass fed dressed up like a caterer tryin' to plant a bug in the don's kitchen. Laziness breeds predictability."

"Shift changes."

"For a second-rate writer and a third-rate insurance man, you surprise me," was his backhanded compliment. "These guys must eat prune and oat bran pasta they're so fuckin' regular." He looked at his watch. "Do you still carry that extra gas can in your bug?"

"Yeah," I was having a wave of second thoughts.

"Good. This is what I want you to do. In fifteen minutes . . ."

The plan made sense if you liked stunt work and exploding Volkswagens. I'd never done any stunt work and since it was my Volkswagen scheduled to go up in flames, you could understand my trepidation. I was supposed to pull my old bug up to the front gate during the changing of the guard, come staggering away from the car, count to five and run like hell back down the hill. It was MacClough's responsibility to hit the extra gas can shoved into the VW's engine compartment. After I'd set the world's record for the downhill run and my car went boom, Johnny and I would rendezvous at the soft spot in the perimeter security. From there, I was just supposed to shut up and follow.

"How'd you find out about the hole in their defense?" I asked, regressing to football terminology.

"I got a friend on the job that had the Gandolfo surveillance detail for five years. He knows the grounds better than the fuckin' landscapers."

"Do we have to blow up my car?"

"If ya wanna play, ya gotta pay," Johnny offered up like a bad Lotto commercial. He checked his watch again. "Okay, let's get goin'. It'll take a minute to get that gas can wedged in there."

"See ya."

We shook hands and I turned for the hole in the hedges. I'd put about two yards between us when snow at my back crunched beneath someone else's feet. There was a silent eternity in the instant between those footsteps and the slamming collapse of my skull. After the long journey to earth in that shadow moment between unconsciousness and light, the snow felt strangely warm against my cheek. Johnny knelt down next to me, checked my eyes and the sore spot where his gun butt landed. I could see his lips were moving, but the snapping of flames searing my brain drowned out MacClough's words. I'd like to think he was telling me I'd live and that a concussion was worth it if it meant I could keep my Volkswagen. He was more likely calling me a guillible prick. And if he wasn't, he should have. I didn't try to speak and when I saw Johnny disappear behind some trees, I closed my eyes and wandered into the moonless night of dreams.

Dead Sea Scrolls

I opened my stubborn eyes. The calico cat had returned and was sniffing at my chin. When she noticed my eyes flicker, she skittered back a bit and decided to watch the show from a safe distance. I knew there would be pain, but when I lifted off the snow an inch or two, I convulsed slightly. That scared me and like an overmatched pug I tried convincing myself to stay down for the count. I didn't listen.

I sat back on my knees without retching or convulsing, but I did have the shakes real bad. It was still nighttime and, by the look of the moon, not too much time had elapsed since MacClough had given me the pill. I had neglected to wear a watch. Writers don't need watches. I could make out the shape of my VW thru the bushes. It wasn't the chariot of fire envisioned in Johnny's diversionary plan. The only thing diverted had been me.

I pushed to stand and went cogwheel stiff with pain. I crashed, my face landing bull's-eye in the snow. God, wasn't this fun? I got back on my knees and washed my head with snow. I rinsed my mouth out with some and swallowed a bit. It tasted like the wind smelled; laced with sulphur and hydrocarbons and refinery fumes. But it was cold and wet and its flavor helped clear the cobwebs.

The cat moved closer. I put a mildly shaky hand down to pet her. She sniffed at my finger, rubbed her cheek against it and purred. I stood up and waited for the earthquake to subside before taking a step. And when the

ground beneath my feet slowed from a rolling boil to a
light simmer, I went on.

MacClough deceived me about turning my car into a
Roman candle and had sapped me down. I was hoping
that's where the lies would end, because I was headed for
that weak link in the security chain. I looked for my feline
amigo, but she had split. Her delicate paws leaving a trail
of flowers in the snow. I guess she had no stomach for my
stupidity.

I picked up MacClough's footprints almost immediately. The moonlight helped. There was no attempt on his
part to cover the tracks—no branch brushing or doubling
back—and they seemed to be headed in the direction the
ex-detective had described. With each step I gained confidence that Johnny hadn't lied about the soft spot in Fort
Gandolfo, but with my rising confidence came rising
doubts. I still had no plan, no idea of what to do when I
arrived at the hole in the net. And the closer I got, the
more I liked the plan with which I'd been deceived. There
was something to be said for shutting up and following
the leader.

The soft spot was no lie. About ten paces to my left
stood the double-trunk tree which would be my bridge
across the high stone wall topped in wrought iron fleurs-
de-lis. Vlad the Impaler came immediately to mind. On
the Gandolfo side of the wall, I could also see the kids'
treehouse John had mentioned as a landing zone. In Ore-
gon, kids climb trees. In Brooklyn, we climbed wire
fences and fire escapes. And I was no whiz with those.
Now I was supposed to climb up the double-trunk tree,
slither out onto an overhanging limb and jump onto the
roof of the playhouse. Added to the fact that I would never
be a threat to Tarzan or Sir Edmund Hillary, were the
elements of snow, darkness, metal spears and my concussion. Somehow, it'd all seemed easier when MacClough
had laid it out.

For what it's worth, I actually whispered: "Geronimo!"

It wasn't worth much. I missed, skidding off the treehouse roof, tumbling through branches and landing on my left shoulder. I suppose the cushion of snow prevented me from breaking it. Shit, maybe it was broken, but I was too busy rolling around from the pain in my skull to give it much serious consideration.

After doing my second snow bath in the last fifteen minutes, my shoulder started to hurt badly. When I wind-milled my left arm a bit to try and relieve the distress, the shoulder down to my fingertips went numb. I wouldn't be doing much tree climbing for awhile. I didn't need a plan now, since I couldn't get out the way I'd come in. I looked for the lights of the main house and headed in that direction. I was hoping to get there before being shot. And short of actually being killed, I prayed that no one would ask me to put my hands up.

No one shot me, stabbed me or asked for loose change. Clearly, this was nothing like a walk in Manhattan. I only had the wind to keep me company as I crossed the grounds. Apparently, the Gandolfos' taste did not run to full-scale models of ancient English ruins; nor was a visitor likely to fall prey to an attack by mutant plaster religious figures. At worst, a guest might cramp up in the marble swimming pool or twist an ankle on the tennis court. I looked for a bocci green, but couldn't see one in all the snow. I passed a cabana, a tool shed and a monster garage; each easily larger than the apartment I grew up in. Hell, the garage could have accommodated the QE 2, but I bet they never used it for anything larger than a 747. They did use its girth to hide a satellite dish certainly the equal of Ping Pong Palermo's.

The main house was nothing to write home about. It was larger than the garage, but smaller than the palace at Versailles. In fact, the three-floored colonial looked rather plain for a Mafia don's villa. I'd expected something along the lines of the Jefferson Memorial or the Pantheon. Now I stood just five feet away from sliding glass doors which ran midway along the colonial's pool-facing back wall. The indoor side of the glass doors was heavily curtained, but not so heavily that I couldn't make out light fighting through the drapery. And upon close inspection, I saw that the far left door was open a crack. I didn't like it. I didn't like the open door policy. I didn't like having gotten this far, unencumbered. I knew prostitutes that weren't this easy. This wasn't a soft spot in security. This wasn't security at all. This was an invitation. And I accepted.

"Glad you could join the party, Mr. Klein," an unfamiliar voice welcomed me. It's owner was hidden somewhere behind an expansive mahogany bar. "Pat him down, Vinny," the voice carelessly commanded and then wondered absentmindedly: "Where's the black Sambuca?"

Across the bar, seated on a green leather and brass tacked sofa was MacClough. He was bleeding from the nose and mouth and his right eye was swollen shut. Behind him stood a stone-faced fireplug of a man in his fifties wearing an ugly brown polyester suit. He had old school written all over him. He was the type that killed to keep in practice and, unlike Vinny, wouldn't mind taking some lumps in the process. When Johnny acknowledged my presence by leaning forward, Fireplug rapped him with the back of his hand. "Stop bleedin' on the fuckin' couch."

Vinny the lisping Adonis started to frisk me. "You look like shit."

"Where's your bosth?" I asked, mimicking the muscle head.

"He'th not carrying, don Roberto," Vinny announced with slave-like reverence.

And suddenly I understood Larry Feld's caveat about the old man.

"Here it is," a deeply tanned, bald head popped up from behind the bar. Its face displayed a sweet, grandfatherly demeanor, but its eyes were traitors to the mask. They were morgue-room black; cruel, cold and detached. They were the eyes of a dangerous man, even more dangerous than the eyes of his son.

I took a quick step toward MacClough, but that's as close as I would get. Vinny clamped a finger vise around my neck and I went stiff with pain. I nearly fainted.

"Vinny, Vinny," the old don came running around the bar, "is that anyway to treat a guest?" Don Roberto held a glass of inky black liquid under my nose. It's licorice smell made me dry-retch. Don Roberto didn't like that, pulled the glass away and slapped me across the face.

"Thanks, I needed that," I smiled. So did Don Roberto.

"I'm sorry to disappoint you and Detective MacClough, but—"

"Retired," Johnny interrupted just to bust balls.

"Shut up!" Fireplug clapped MacClough's left ear and put him to sleep.

"As I was sayin'," his Brooklyn was starting to show, "I'm sorry to disappoint you, but my son won't be joinin' us tonight. Always busy, my son. Always busy with the *puttana*. You know what *puttana* is, Mr. Klein?"

"Whore," I replied.

"Where you learn that?" the old man seemed genuinely impressed.

"Brighton Beach. Half the kids in my high school were named Cohen and the other half were named Carbone."

"Cohen and Carbone. Hey Vinny, I like that. Cheech," the don turned to Fireplug and uttered something in Italian.

In the next instant, Vinny and the old school soldier were carrying MacClough into another room. Don Roberto was so comfortable with his power and so certain of it, that he didn't bother threatening me or warning me about trying to escape. He just knew I'd stay put. He was right.

"My son is a weak man, Mr. Klein."

"Not according to the newspapers and TV," I interrupted now that the muscle was out of the room. It didn't matter. The old man wouldn't be derailed. "He stinks of fish, my son. A man should find a wife. If he wants to have fun, he takes a mistress. We understand that. But not my son. No. Ever since that cunt turned against him," Don Roberto was shouting now, spraying my face with spit, "he's been a waste to me and this family. I should have been able to enjoy my painting, my opera . . . Instead, I must pull the strings. Always, I must pull the strings. We have people to take care of, responsibilities."

"*You* had her whacked," it was almost a whisper. "*You* had Azrael killed."

Robby "the Boot" smiled with his fine white teeth and crooked lips, but his eyes were unwaveringly chilly. "No, Mr. Klein, I didn't have anything done to that whore who preferred a cop to my Dante. I had the pleasure of carrying out *la vendetta* myself. My only regrets were that I could not have made her pain last longer and that I had to waste a perfectly good canary."

"But I found a freshly buried body out in a field near Sound Hill."

"*You* found the body! Fuckin' incompetent cops," don Roberto threw his thin arms to heaven. "That stiff was a little Christmas present," the old man crossed himself, "from me to them."

"You killed a man just to throw the cops off the trail?" I guess I sounded naive to the Mafia king.

"These things happen," was his calm response as if he was explaining to his wife that the dog had eaten her rose bush. "Anyway, he was a cruel man. The world will not mourn him."

"But why after all this time?" I asked.

"Do you like a beer, Mr. Klein?" He answered my question with one of his own.

"Sure."

The don offered me a frosted bottle of Peroni. I would have prefered a Corona, an Anchor Steam or even a Budweiser, but the situation called for diplomacy and I accepted the Italian beer with a nod. It went down smoothly enough and was a definite improvement over polluted snow. The don took a bottle for himself.

"What do you think of my bar?" Robby "the Boot" was just full of questions.

"A little big for the room," I burped and excused myself, "but it's fine work." I wondered where this was leading.

"It's from one of Capone's speaks. One day outta the blue, I get a call from a guy I haven't heard from in years. He tells me he bought this bar in a junk yard in Connecticut and he can't unload it and he's gonna have to sell it for firewood and he knows I have an eye for fine carpentry. I tell the guy I'll think about it, but first he gotta answer some questions: How much for the piece? How much kickback does he get? How many people was it offered to before me? And why didn't they take it?" the don took a gulp of beer and made a disapproving face.

"Well, Mr. Klein," he continued, "this dealer could answer all of those questions but one. The price was right. Damn cheap, if you ask me. This guy says he's willing to take half his usual finder's fee just to get rid of the piece and he gives me the name of everyone it's been offered to. But he can't explain why no one's taken the deal."

"You took it."

"I did," the old man slapped the bar, "but not because it was from a Capone speak or because I loved it. You're right, it's too big for the room. When I look at this bar, it makes me wonder about why people do or don't do things they should. That's a good thing to think about in my business." I had a funny feeling we were about to get to the point.

"A few months ago, I get another call."

"Antique dealer?" I busted his balls a little.

"Cop. Dirty cop. Used to be a bag man for me."

"O'Toole," I took a not so wild guess.

"Smart," don Roberto gave me the crooked smile. "Jews are so fuckin' smart. No wonder the rest of the fuckin' planet can't stand 'em."

"That's a point."

"So this donkey tells us he's found Dante's old *puttana* and that for the right price not only can he tell me where to find her, but he can drive her into my backyard. I don't like it, becuse he shouldn't be calling me. To the rest of the world, it's my son that runs things. No one should have to come to me. And when I ask him why he did, he—"

"O'Toole tells you that you're *not* the first person he's come to," I sipped on my beer and paused, "but the last."

"That prick, O'Toole. He says he's talked to everyone in the organizattion about that bitch and they all promise to pass the word on. Only no one gets back to him. He has the stones to ask me if the Gandolfos are getting soft. And he wonders how that will play out on the street," the don's face grew pink under his luxurious tan and his expression turned as sour as month-old milk. "I sat there and listened to this potato-eating piece of shit insult my family. This moron who couldn't wipe his ass without written instructions is spitting in my face."

"But you checked O'Toole's story out just to make sure," I put the empty beer bottle down, "and it turns out he's telling the truth. Dante could have gotten Azrael for months, but sat on the information instead. And you came down here and looked at that bar and wondered why. None of the explanations you came up with satisfied you. Did they?" I asked rhetorically. "So you took O'Toole up on his offer and killed the woman to punish your son and to make sure word wouldn't get around that the Gandolfos were going soft. Then you whacked O'Toole for insulting your honor and to clean up any loose ends. All very neat."

"I didn't touch O'Toole," Roberto Gandolfo looked at me with fierce displeasure. "Don't ever insult me like that again."

Talk about surreal. Here's a man that just got done telling me he murdered a woman and was sorry only that he couldn't make the hurt last long enough, a man who murdered someone else just to throw the cops a red herring and he's mad that I implied he might have killed someone who actually deserved it. Silly me.

"Never again. Scout's honor," was what I said. "Can I ask you something, don Roberto?"

He nodded I could.

"What was the canary business all about? It's a little old-fashioned."

"So am I, Mr. Klein. But the bird was a message to my son, so he would understand who had taken his *puttana* away."

I thought about asking the don why he just didn't discuss the matter with his son, but I was understandably shy about insulting him.

"Cheech!" Don Roberto shouted at the walls and the stocky man appeared almost instantaneously. "Now that you've rested and finished your beer, Mr. Klein," the old man's eyes captured mine, "the time has come to save your life and your friend's."

"I thought you people didn't kill cops and civilians," my voice broke.

"Yeah, and in the big war we only bombed military targets," he enjoyed his own sarcasm. "It's nice to see a grown man who still believes in the tooth fairy. Anyway, who said *I* was gonna kill you? I know a few spics and gooks who aren't so choosy about who they stick their shivs into as long as the money's right."

"So what can I do for you?" I asked, feeling suddenly weak-legged and light-headed. I wasn't so naive as to think I'd ever see the sun again, even if I had the answers he wanted.

"My boy is soft like a little girl, Mr. Klein. Only once before has he been disloyal to his family. I knew the details then. I don't know them now. By not coming to me about that bitch, Dante put in jeopardy my whole organization. My guts tell me you know what secret that *puttana* held over my son's head."

Soft like a little girl, huh? To this guy, soft like a little girl meant you hadn't slaughtered as many people as Attila the Hun and you hadn't enjoyed it as much as Jack the Ripper.

"Did you ever think of asking your son?"

The don gave his head a quick twist and with that, Cheech put a granite fist into my right kidney. I went down like the Titanic.

"I warned you about insulting me, Mr. Klein," he slapped my face for good measure. "Roberto Gandolfo does not crawl to his son, *capisce*?"

In between gasps for air, I nodded that I understood.

"I've also spoken to my attorney," my inquisitor added.

"Fuck Larry Feld," I coughed. Cheech rapped a knuckle into the bump on my head which had risen since Johnny's gun butt had kissed it.

"Mr. Feld tells me you've been very interested in these goings-on for a long time. And you know what else?" He neglected to wait for my reply. "My lawyer says you had a meeting with my son and that you received a hundred large to give to a dead whore. That's a curious thing, Mr. Klein."

"Very," I agreed from my standard kneeling position.

"One more time, Mr. Klein, I ask you nicely. What was the *puttana* holding over Dante's head for all these years?"

I never really considered telling him about Leyna. He didn't deserve to know. And as long as I knew something the Mafia king did not, my chances to continue breathing were enhanced.

"I don't know what you're talking about."

"You got big balls," don Roberto complimented, "but I don't give out medals for big balls."

The senior Gandolfo twisted his head again. This time Cheech gave it to me in both kidneys full out. As my face touched carpet, the flavors of iron and salt mixed in my mouth with the remnants of hops and barley. In my waning seconds of consciousness, I heard a feverish exchange, mostly in Italian, between the old man and his rude boy. Unfortunately, the few words I could make out were Vinny, cop, tool shed, wood chipper and snow blower. Even in my diminished state, I could divine that putting a positive spin on what I'd just overheard would be only slightly harder than deciphering the Dead Sea Scrolls.

A motorcycle gang of hornets buzzed in my ears and my nose breathed in their exhaust. My cheek and beard were very wet and when I cranked my eyes open, I noticed my pillow was a shallow puddle, my bed a concrete floor. MacClough was next to me, bloody-faced and face up, breathing very heavily through his battered mouth. I was trapped between my desire to survey the surroundings and yet maintained the outward appearance of unconsciousness. I compromised, swiveling my sore eyes around as far as they'd go.

The hornets were not bees at all nor were the fumes and metal chatter the by-products of idling Harley Davidsons. About five yards past the top of Johnny's head, I saw an impressive display of yard care equipment, one piece of which was revved up and ready to go. Unfortunately, this wasn't a John Deere showroom and I was fairly certain no one on the premises had midnight lawn care in mind.

"Hey!" a big paw grabbed me by the collar, dragged me over to the machinery and stood me up. Vinny was my dancing partner. I guess he liked to lead. Cheech did a similar tango with MacClough. Robby "the Boot" bounced on over, doing an excited little tarantella. Gee, how festive the promise of torture made everyone.

Vinny put me in a head lock and towed my stiff torso over to the iron mouth of the wood chipper. The old don joined us there, took out a straight razor and slit my left sleeve up to the shoulder. Musclehead switched holds and clamped my bare arm, forcing it to fully extend. I began to struggle. That only seemed to excite my dancing partner. Good thing I didn't beg or he just might've come in his pants.

Roberto Gandolfo cupped my wet beard in a cold, bony hand. "Your friend came here to kill me, Mr. Klein. That I cannot forgive."

"Yeah, and what was that song and dance before about saving my life and his?" I was stalling. The thought of having my arm food processed while I was awake and still attached to it gave me sufficient motivation to stall.

"A white lie, Mr. Klein," he gave my face an affectionate pat. "Please forgive me. Now your choice is a different one. I will keep you alive until you tell me what secret my son was willing to jeopardize this organization for, but life can be very painful. You and the cop can go peacefully or in pieces. The decision is yours."

"Can you give me thirty years to think about it?"

"No, but I can help you understand your situation better," the old don moved his hands away from my face. "Vinny, help Mr. Klein."

My arm was in the chipper's throat before the echo of the don's voice had stopped pinging around the corrugated steel building. I could feel the wind of the blades blowing back the hair along my forearm. I balled my hand reflexively, but too late to save the tip of my index finger. There was no immediate pain, but the realization gave me a burst of strength to retard the chipper's appetite and to knock Vinny slightly off balance. When the pain did come, someone screamed. I noticed it was me.

MacClough, feigning unconsciousness till that point, caught Cheech enjoying the show and broke free of the fireplug's grip. Naturally distracted by Johnny's charge,

Vinny eased his hold on me and braced himself to absorb MacClough's blow. I pulled my left arm free of the dragon's teeth and drove the back of my head into Vinny's nose. I went down, squeezing what remained of my left forefinger in my right hand. MacClough's shoulder dug deep into Vinny's ribs. The pony-tailed bodyguard stumbled, throwing a careless arm out for balance. It was the last time he'd throw that arm out for anything ever again.

The chipper made fast work of the muscle boy's appendage, spitting out bits of bone and flesh against a corner of the shed. The machine, however, did not seem satiated by Vinny's arm. Apparently, his leather blazer had got caught up in the blades and the chipper used it to pull its quarry further and further in. Eventually the teeth bit into something they could not digest and the blades stopped churning. The old man rushed to shut the chipper off, but he was way too late. The bodyguard's legs hung limply as a rubber chicken's from the mouth of the machine.

Cheech was literally sitting on MacClough's back, holding his 9 millimeter to Johnny's ear.

"Shit!" morgue-eyes slammed the chipper and actually kicked the soles of Vinny's dead feet. "*Stunad*! Idiot!"

"See what happens when you don't pay attention in metal shop," MacClough chided and was rewarded by having his face scraped along the concrete floor.

"Kill them," the raving man yelled at Cheech. "Kill them both now." And when the somewhat startled soldier didn't immediately blow a hole in Johnny MacClough's brain, Don Roberto took a wild run at him, slapped the hard guy twice across the face and relieved him of his automatic.

"But Don Roberto," Cheech offered meekly. "Not a cop. Not here."

It was sound advice, but the old man wasn't having any and pointed the confiscated gun at MacClough's shredded face.

"Stop Papa," Dante Gandolfo's voice rang in my ears

like a cavalry bugle blowing 'Charge!' "Enough Papa, enough." The son strode into view, an automatic pistol in his paw to match the one his father held. Larry Feld walked up right behind the junior Gandolfo.

"Someone take a picture," the elder gunman mimed a photographer with his free hand. "I need proof. Mr. Klein," unfortunately Don Roberto remembered I was still alive. "Do you see this? My son has never made his bones like a real man and he points a gun at his father. It's to laugh, no?"

"You're wrong Papa. I've made my bones. Quite recently, but I guess killing a man counts no matter when you do it."

I could swear the old man's face took on a prideful countenance.

"O'Toole," I blurted out my favorite answer for the evening.

"Don't respond to that, Dante," Larry counseled.

"Shut up, Larry," Don Juan rejected. "That's right, Mr. Klein. He deserved to die for going to my father about Azrael. And then he tried blackmailing me."

"Blackmail?" I hung the question on the line to dry.

"What blackmail?" the old man asked scornfully. "What did that donkey prick threaten you with? Do you think I don't know about you and that cunt reporter from the *Times* and how you were her pipeline to us? Good thing for her, the bottom fell out."

Roberto "the Boot" couldn't have known it, but his venomous disclosure had just answered a whole set of questions I had on another matter. It also reaffirmed, to everyone's relief, that he had no inkling of Azarel's daughter.

Dante Gandolfo went white, his gun tip dropping slightly. "How did you know about the *Times* thing? How Papa?"

"Do you think that I have lived this long by not know-

ing things? I know what I have to know. Do you think I
hired that idiot stickin' outta the machine just to drive
your car?" We all took another look at Vinny's rubber
legs. In a few hours we'd be able to use them as parallel
bars. "What does it matter, Dante?" his father continued.
"You're like clockwork. Every ten years you try to destroy me. All I have to do is check the calendar and wait
for you to hurt me. But no more. I'm glad to have killed
that old bitch of yours. Too bad I couldn't have done it
before she taught *you* how to sing. That bird in her mouth
was a present for you."

Don Juan's gun hand was shaking now. That wasn't
good news for Johnny. The shakes don't exactly make for
good aim and if the old don made a move to kill Mac-
Clough, there was no way Dante could have stopped him
with one bullet. I had to try something.

"You're a man who needs to know things," I shouted
at Don Roberto from my concrete chair. "That need cost
me a finger," I held the still seeping stump up for inspection. "But I've always been bad at holding a grudge, so
I'm gonna tell you what you need to know."

"Shut up!" MacClough gurgled through the blood.

"Don't!" Don Juan chimed in, almost stepping on the
ex-cop's plea.

"You got any grandchildren, Don Roberto?" I asked,
slipping on my own blood as I got to my feet.

"No," the old man choked out as if he'd swallowed a
piece of glass. "That is yet another way in which my son
has failed me."

"Wrong, Don Roberto." The room got quiet enough
now to hear the amber lights buzz above our heads.
"You've got a granddaughter. And what you need to
know is that you killed her mother in the snow and cold
of Christmas Eve."

MacClough had told me he wasn't sure who the father

had been, but this wasn't the time to quibble over details. Besides, everyone in the shed, except Cheech, thought I knew more than I did.

"Tell me he's lying, Dante," father ordered son.

The latter stayed silent.

"Tell me he's lying," the old man swung the gun up from Johnny and pointed the 9 millimeter at my heart. "Tell me, Dante. Tell me." His trigger finger twitched.

Two shots snapped the tension, their reports echoed and amplified by the metal walls and concrete. The old don's neck exploded like an overripe watermelon and he hit the deck with a skull-cracking thud. I don't think he felt the fall. The gun in his dying hand shot the second bullet into Vinny's ignorant left thigh, showering me in the by-products of ballistic impact. Cheech lay down on top of Johnny, and Larry Feld grabbed some floor. Dante Gandolfo just stood there, looking at the cool barrel of his gun. I imagine he wanted to confirm he hadn't fired the fatal shot.

"Police," a bored voice announced as if he'd repeated the word so many times it hurt. "Just everybody relax and no one else'll spring a leak."

Larry Feld popped up like an unwanted pimple and began explaining to the cops that his client was licensed to carry a handgun in New York City and that he would have no statement this evening. Cheech ran like a loyal dog to its fallen master, cradling the old man's lifeless head in his polyester lap. I could see MacClough's face from where I stood and he placed a vertical finger across his scabbed and swollen lips. I understood. Sirens became the world's dominant sound. I was glad to hear them because my ex-finger was starting to hurt like hell.

"Klein! God, you look like shit," Detective Mickelson critiqued, holstering his .38. "I got concerned when you didn't show to claim your jacket."

"A little outta your jurisdiction," I noted, my muscles contracting from pain. "Who plugged the don?"

"One of the city boys. Like you said, I'm out of my jurisdiction."

"I'll have to thank him for saving my ass," I leaned against Buddha belly to stop myself from falling. "How'd'ya know where to find me?"

"Let's just say I've been reading the same book as you, only I was a few pages behind. Now let's get a doctor to look at that finger," the Suffolk cop deflected.

"No!" I pulled away. "How'd ya know to show up here, now, just when you did?"

His eyes scanned the building until they were focused directly on the back of Larry Feld's head. And when Mickelson was certain I'd taken note of his stare, he said: "Phone tip. Anonymous, of course."

"Of course," I seconded.

So the tip had come from Larry Feld. I could never confront him about it, because he would never confess to it. For the first time in my life, I couldn't see the self-interest in what he'd done. I don't know. Maybe it was the phone conversation we'd had earlier. I hadn't pressured him directly, but rather talked about the old block and the de facto friends we knew and how they'd all disappeared. I talked about his joyless parents and how I'd always known he was as much a victim of Auschwitz as they. I reminded him of the Irish kids kicking our Jewish asses on the way home from synagogue on Saturday mornings. I'd like to think I appealed to whatever humanity there was in Larry Feld, but I would never really know.

All of us refused to make anything but the vaguest of statements that evening. The doctors insulated both Johnny and me from any curious law enforcement officials and the press. Dante Gandolfo had previously, through his lawyer, made it clear that he wouldn't be speaking to anyone until after his father's funeral. And Cheech, the old school soldier that he was, refused to give the cops his name let alone a statement.

Before they loaded us into the ambulance, I had a few
parting words with Detective Mickelson.

"You know that book we're both reading . . ." I
drifted.

"Yeah."

"Can you give me a few days before you discuss it with
anyone else?"

"You know I can't guarantee that," he stated calmly,
"but there are a few parts of the book I don't see as being
of general interest."

"What parts might those be?"

"I think we both know the answer to that. Don't we,
Detective Bosco?" he shook his head disapprovingly. "If
people are interested in those parts of the story, they can
read the book for themselves. Good night, Mr. Klein.
Your jacket will be waiting for you in my office." He
slammed the ambulance door shut.

MacClough had used some of his old cop charm and
connections to insure we were alone in the back of the
sick wagon. I guess we had some important things to
talk about. But as we pulled away from the gates of Fort
Gandolfo, Johnny seemed to be out of it. I looked out of
the ambulance back window and noticed that we were just
passing the late Paul Palermo's estate. This was a different
view from the one I'd seen in my earlier approach, yet
even from here I could make out the circle of painted
plaster Marys. I couldn't help but ponder what the sig-
nificance of these statues was. Maybe, I thought, they
were like Don Roberto's mahogany bar; something for a
powerful man to stare at and wonder why. They certainly
made me wonder.

"Dylan," MacClough's strained voice broke the trance.

"You're up." I had a gift for the self-evident.

"Yeah, I noticed that, too."

"How do you feel?" I knelt down next to him.

"About as good as the tip of your fuckin' finger. How
do you think I feel?"

"Stupid question. Listen, we got to get some stuff straightened out before we get to the hospital. I think I know where—"

"I don't wanna know, Klein. I don't wanna know where she is and I don't want anyone else to know. I'm sure she's had enough hurt in her life. She doesn't need to catch any more. The curse died with Azrael. Let it stay that way. Just make sure she gets the hundred grand."

I thought of a thousand reasonable things to say against the course MacClough had chosen, but said none of them. This part *was* his business and somewhere in the pulp of my bone marrow, I even understood.

"It's Gandolfo's money."

"Nevermind about him," Johnny assured me. "He won't ask for it back."

"Listen," I shifted gears, "if you want me to protect Azrael's daughter, I need you to do something for me. You gotta get Kate Barnum in to see me tomorrow before I talk to the cops."

His puffed and bruised face puzzled at the request, but all he said was that he could probably manage it. Apparently, injured detectives, even retired ones, pulled a lot of weight.

"Here," he yanked his hand free from under the restraining straps and dropped something onto my right palm. It was a white gold and diamond confection. I counted twenty-four stones aligned like stars in the shape of a heart. Each gem rested in the petrified fingers of white gold hands. "Make sure she gets this, too." And having finally let go of the heart, Johnny Blue closed his eyes to sleep.

Prepayment

The trauma unit orthopedist visited my bedside and rambled on about the median nerve, radialis indicis, abductors, phalanges and occupational therapy. When pressed for a translation, he said I'd lost the top of my left index finger and there wasn't a whole hell of a lot he could do about it. He went on to say that there'd been considerable damage to the traumatized area and that I should consider myself fortunate that he didn't need to remove more tissue. After witnessing Vinny's metamorphosis from bodyguard to shark chum, I found the doctor's little pep talk about good fortune anticlimactic. When I mentioned that my former finger really didn't hurt much, he assured me it wouldn't last. How comforting.

The rest of me wasn't in much better shape than my finger. Thanks to Cheech's fondness for my kidneys, I'd been pissing more blood than urine. My left shoulder was mildly separated and my nearly healed ribs were sore again. There was a bump on my head big enough to be sculpted into the likeness of a dead president and I had a headache twice that size. I tried not thinking about how MacClough might be feeling. I didn't have the stomach for it.

Kate Barnum walked in as if gravity could no longer hold her down. And who could blame her. This was resurrection day, her own little Easter. I'd once said that she'd never be considered good looking. Today I was wrong. There was order to the tangle of her hair and the make-up was miraculously right. An unclasped, black leather trenchcoat replaced the usual dirty down jacket. A fiery silk blouse covered her breasts. Pleated, gray flannel pants played off beautifully against the heat of her shirt. Her boots and belt were a match for the coat. I wasn't missing her frayed sweaters, cut sweatshirts or blue jeans just now. My hospital room smelled like a tannery next door to a perfume shop.

We did not speak. My erection was fairly evident to both of us. Without pretense or wasted motion, Kate dropped her coat where she stood, pulled back my covering sheet and sat facing me across my bare legs. The hospital gown fairly fell away. Neither one of us gave much thought to being caught by the police guard outside my door.

She came forward and ran her tongue along the underside of my penis, using her right thumb and forefinger to lightly circle and brush the tip. When enough saliva to prevent chaffing had collected, she encircled me, moving her hand slowly; tightly down, softly up. Barnum placed her O-shaped lips atop her right hand and let them go along for the ride. Her free left hand slid to her own waist, carefully undoing both belt and buttons. The hand disappeared from view. The reporter's calf muscles tightened around my thighs, her breathing became labored and irregular.

My head was spinning from pain, lack of blood and air. The base of my diminished finger pulsated at the same rhythm as my heart. Something wet tugged down my bottom lip and slipped through my teeth. Kate had presented me a sample of herself and I took it, moving along her finger just as she moved along me. I rocketed into her mouth and lost consciousness for a time, a short time.

We did not kiss or caress and there were no shy, guilty glances. Sex between Kate and me was about many things, but never affection. It was ritual. It was barter. It was code. It was hollow as humping a ghost. Today it was a gift from a goddess, an apology, a farewell, a prepayment of sorts for services rendered and stories to be told.

I lay in bed looking like a half-peeled potato while Barnum pulled a chair up alongside. Her mini-recorder was next to me and running. She had a pad in her lap and chewed on a cheap pen that she wished was a Chesterfield.

Kate Barnum had waited a long time for the story that would lift her from the ashes, but she'd have to be patient a bit longer while I decided how I wanted to do what I had to do. I decided to ask my questions first.

"Did O'Toole come to you or did you go to him?"

I could see her trying the costume of denial on for size. I guess she decided it didn't fit.

"It was a combination of both," she admitted, exhaling with relief. "Let's just say we had a marriage of convenience."

"Was he the one who introduced you to Dante Gandolfo?"

Now her face went cold. Kate Barnum didn't expect anyone to know about Gandolfo being her source for that series on the Mafia. She began to shape her lips into a question, but I made a preemptive strike.

"Listen Kate, I'm gonna give you your story," I shut her recorder off. "But you're partially responsible for three, maybe four people's deaths and for a lot of pain." I held up my bandaged hand. "I wanna know how the fuck the chain reaction started."

"You get to meet a lot of cops when you do what I do. Even if you don't write crime stuff, cops are always around people who make the news." Barnum picked up her coat and patted down the pockets for cigarettes that weren't there. "You get to know some of them pretty well. You go for a drink with one and he introduces you to another one."

"That's how you met O'Toole."

"Yeah, I'd been at the *Times* for a few months, and this

cop I was going around with introduced me to O'Toole.
No big thing," she smirked. "Then, years later, I get a call
from him. I didn't even remember who he was. But he
remembered me, all right. Whores are like that. He says
the word on the street is that I'm looking for dirt on the
Gandolfos and that he knows someone who might be willing to talk to me."

"How much did it cost you?" I pulled the cover sheet
back over me.

"Who said anything about money?"

"Whores are like that," I fed her own words back.
"Now come on. I know you. I met him. And the *Times*
doesn't pay for stories. What did it cost you?"

"About everything I had, but it was worth it."

"To have the son of the most powerful crime boss in
America as a source. Yeah, I bet it was worth it," I
coughed. "Ever wonder why Don Juan was willing to
spill?"

"It's the one thing he wouldn't discuss, but most sons
don't rat out their fathers unless it's got something to do
with hate and revenge." She went cigarette searching
again. "Besides, I didn't really care."

"Not until much later."

Barnum nodded in agreement. "Not until much later."

"So Dante Gandolfo starts slowly, giving you bits and
pieces. He can't afford to give you too much too soon and
risk being found out. You meet a union official here, a
button man there and you're startin' to build a nice foun-
dation for your series. Then your husband swallows half
the medicine cabinet and that's that. Good-bye sources.
Good-bye stories. Good-bye career."

She winced when I mentioned her husband, following
that with distant eyes and a cautious smile. Kate Barnum
hadn't expected me to know some of the things I did.
That made her wonder about what else I might know and
who else might know it.

"Okay, that's old news." I didn't want to spook her so

much that she'd clam up. "Let's time travel to the more recent past."

"Ben Vandermeer's more of a father to me than my own, but do you have any idea what working at the *Whaler* is like for me?"

"Sort of like being the bullpen catcher for Oneonta."

"What?" the reporter asked angrily.

"Never mind." I waved her off. "Ben would understand. Go ahead."

"You know about Mike," she said, referring to her late husband, "so I take it you also know about the Pulitzer fiasco."

I shook my head that I did.

"Not a soul in the industry would touch me. I was a leper, a pariah. Oh sure, they were all sorry about Mike, but not one of those sacrosanct, self-righteous hypocrites was willing to let me clean their urinals. Bad for the image, ya know."

"So Ben took you in and you've been hunting for a story you could sell to one of the majors."

"Pretty funny, huh?" Barnum smiled broadly. "Hunting for a major story in Sound Hill's kind of like hunting kangaroos in the Himalayas. Not that it stopped me from trying. I kept in touch with some of my old sources, particularly the ones that didn't require a retainer or up-front money. But even when they came across with something, I either didn't have the resources to do the story right or it wasn't big enough to make it worth my while."

"Until O'Toole called," I suggested.

"Until O'Toole called," she confirmed.

"I think I can guess the rest." The doctor was right. My finger was beginning to burn with pain. "O'Toole says he's come up with an idea that'll make big money for him, create the story you've been looking for and give both of you a measure of revenge against Dante Gandolfo. How'm I doin' so far?"

"I'll stop you when you're about to hit a bump," she

answered, patting down her coat pockets for the third time. "You got a cigarette?"

"Can't smoke it in here anyway." I continued, "I know that O'Toole had been a money mule for the Gandolfos and I assume Dante cut him loose just around the time you got pulled in by the cops. After all, Don Juan couldn't afford any link to you, and O'Toole was a link. So there's his motive for revenge. Your motive runs pretty much along the same lines. Only getting cut off cost you the Pulitzer and your career.

"So O'Toole calls and says he's been looking back over some old copies of the *Times*. That he's got a great-"

"You just hit a bump," she jumped in. "Did O'Toole strike you as an avid *Times* reader? Of course not. Some buddy of his was spending his retirement driving around the country in a Winnebago. Down south somewhere this buddy goes into a grocery store and spots some-one he thinks he remembers as a witness he guarded dur-ing a big trial once, but he's not sure which trial. Cops never stop being cops. On one of his stops back in New York, he looks up O'Toole. You can figure out the rest."

"Pretty amazing coincidence," I smirked.

"Amazing coincidences always happen to other people. When they happen to you, they don't seem so unbeliev-able." She had a point.

"So O'Toole checks it out, gets in touch with you and sets up Azrael's demise. O'Toole assures you that when the fox gets flushed she'll run right to MacClough. How convenient for you that he owned a bar in Sound Hill."

"Another one of those coincidences, I guess," Barnum giggled nervously.

"I guess." I wasn't giggling, nervously or otherwise. "Too bad for you Azrael picked Christmas Eve to come to MacClough. If he'd been working the bar that night, things might've come to a head more rapidly."

"Oh," she said, "I don't know. There were certain benefits to the way things worked out." She put her hand under the sheet and on my thigh.

"Don't insult my intelligence, Kate," I mimicked the late Don Roberto, pushing her hand away. "Don't insult mine and I won't insult yours by asking if you feel guilty about any of this."

"Fair enough," the reporter agreed. "Now that you've got your explanation, when do I get my story?"

"Is now soon enough?" I turned her recorder back on.

I gave it to her from every angle, in baby bites and large chunks. She got an overview and the view from inside my head. She was educated about the smallest details including how I knew most calico cats were female. Ultimately, I told her about Azrael's daughter. She hadn't expected that. O'Toole, having stumbled onto the fact of her existence, was apparently keeping that tidbit for himself. I even suggested that her partner had been using his knowledge of Azrael's daughter to blackmail both Dante Gandolfo and Johnny MacClough. I surmised that O'Toole wanted to squeeze every penny he could out of the situation. Whores, we agreed, were like that. In the end, it was that greed that got him killed.

"I bet you didn't cry when he turned up dead," I offered, bothered by the pain. "He was the only one who could tie you to any of this. And knowing as much about prostitution as you do, you realized it wouldn't be long before he used that advantage to put the bite on you." I rang the nurses' station for some painkillers.

"Yes, Mr. Klein," a distracted West Indian voice responded with all the compassion of a tombstone.

"My finger's killing me."

"Just a few moments, Mr. Klein," was her reply.

Did you ever notice that no matter how modern the hospital is, the intercoms always sound like transistor radios receiving messages from Mars?

Kate Barnum didn't bother addressing my conclusions about O'Toole's passing from this earth. She just wanted me to hurry up and finish. And I obliged. I was, after all, a man of my word. After a few minor questions about minor details, she put her pad away and reached for her recorder. I slammed my hand down on top of hers.

The reporter didn't have to ask with words. Her eyes did it for her.

"You got your story, Kate," I yanked the recorder open and popped out its little cassette, "but it'll never make it to print."

"You bastard! Give me that," she lunged at the tape and missed.

I unspooled the cassette and wrapped the freed tape around my bandaged hand.

"I don't need that," Barnum got up, straightening her blouse, "and I don't need you."

"If you print a word of it, we'll all deny it. You won't have a bit of corroborative evidence. And considering your previous misfortune with fabricated sources, I'd say you needed me very badly," I confidently concluded.

"You're a smug one, aren't you, Dylan?" she asked, patting down her coat pockets yet again. "Do you recognize this?" Barnum didn't produce a Chesterfield, but rather my safe deposit box key. "You should never underestimate me, Dylan. I knew if you ever found out about my involvement in this, you'd cut me down. And you might've been successful if you hadn't gotten all dramatic and gone running to Ben."

"Ben?"

"That old fart's been in love with me since I was sixteen." Her spirit soared again. "A twenty-five year crush will undo professional ethics faster than a speeding bullet. As a matter of fact, that's about how long it took him to come."

I shook my head in disbelief.

"What are you shaking your head about?"

"That key's worthless," I informed her and without

much joy. "I didn't make it back to the bank on time to hand in the signature card."

"You're bluffing," she tried fighting the good fight.

"Go ahead, try and use the key."

"You cocksucker!" she slapped my face. I grabbed her hand, but after the fact. "I'll print it anyway. I'll print it in the *Whaler* if I have to. I'll drag that dead cunt's daughter through the mud if I have to pull her hair myself."

Holding the ranting woman with my good hand, I fumbled the call button with the other.

"Yes, Mr. Klein. It's a change of shift," the same distracted voice informed. "We'll be getting there as soon as possible."

"Okay, but could you do me a favor?" I was afraid to wait for her answer. "My lawyer is in the visitors' lounge. Can you send him in?"

"Right away, Mr. Klein."

Larry Feld walked in looking tired, but almost gleeful at the prospect of what he was about to do. We'd had a little talk earlier this morning and he agreed that what I was suggesting would be in everybody's best interests. Everybody's, that is, except Kate Barnum's.

"Ms. Barnum," Cassius began cooly, "I have in my hands a document for your inspection. I suggest you read it carefully, but to expedite these proceedings, I shall summarize." I released Barnum's wrist and she snatched the document out of Larry's mitts.

"You will please notice that the document marked 1-A2A, dated this day, is an affidavit, in your name, stating that you shall never, under any circumstance, attempt to discuss and/or publish information concerning the lives of or details pertaining to the lives of the people you see listed there. In return for this guarantee, you shall receive a cash settlement of twenty-five thousand United States dollars."

"You two assholes must be crazy," Kate Barnum turned a ripe tomato shade of red. "I'm not signing away-"

"Ms. Barnum," Larry interrupted, "though it would be a conflict of interest for me to give you legal counsel, I would respectfully suggest you consider what I am about to tell you before rushing to judgment."

"Blah, blah, blah . . ."

"Very well, Ms. Barnum, since you seem disinterested in listening to what I have to say, may I offer you my services, *pro bono* of course, in assisting you in the selection of qualified defense counsel."

"Let's see you try and sue me for libel or slander," Kate Barnum retorted rebelliously.

"I wouldn't think of it, Ms. Barnum. I have the utmost respect for the press and the first amendment rights which protect it from subversion. No, Ms. Barnum, I wasn't discussing a civil action. I was, in fact, discussing murder." I almost yelled: 'Bombs away!' "First degree murder, to be exact."

"Whose, my husband's? You two are really stretching. Don't make me laugh."

"I assure you, miss," Larry could be fatally serious, "that was certainly not my intention. Let me come to the point."

"Do that."

"If you do not sign that document now in your possession within," Feld checked his Rolex, "the next ten minutes, a Suffolk County police officer will arrive at your home armed with a search warrant signed by Judge Robert D. Lockheed. Upon searching the premises, that officer will find a .22 caliber hand gun. The handle will have been wiped clean, but when tested at the lab, the weapon will prove to be the gun used in the recent murder of Terrence O'Toole, N.Y.P.D., retired. I believe you and he were fairly well acquainted."

"You motherfuckers!"

"Sign the affidavit, Ms. Barnum."

"Sign it!" I chimed in.

"Fuck you both," tears were ruining her perfect make-up.

"Sign it, Ms. Barnum. Even the most inept assistant D.A. wouldn't have problems establishing motive, means and opportunity. Sign it!" Larry shoved a Mont Blanc in her face.

She signed it and threw Larry's pen out the window.

The lawyer took the paper from her, checked it and though it killed him to do it, he said: "Thank you. I can now notarize the document. A copy and your check will be delivered to you this evening. And, Ms. Barnum," Larry said, sticking his head back through the door as he was leaving, "if you are contemplating some sort of end run, I'd advise against it. Guns have a nasty habit of disappearing and then reappearing. Also, some of the people I work for are simply nasty. *Capisce?*"

We didn't speak. What was there to say? Both of us began to form words, but only silence came out. We had both done dirty things to one another. I would not take pride in any of them and she could not, not if she had a soul left. If she had, maybe someday it *would* rise again and she could celebrate her little Easter.

"Here's those pills for you, Mr. Klein," a smiling black nurse barged in, carrying a plastic shot cup. "Sorry," she said, noticing the tears on Barnum's cheeks.

"That's okay," I assured her, "the lady was just leaving."

Minute Waltz

Summer was not yet official, but it was that time, late in spring, when the advance troops of the seasonal invaders were beginning to arrive. Harbor traffic had already picked up, as had the prices at the gas station and deli. The Little League parade had since gone by the wayside and the Olde Whaling Fair was just a week up the road. If you've ever wanted a styrofoam harpoon, foam rubber humpback or a membership in Greenpeace, then the fair's the place for you. Sound Hill even dresses up the high school theatre group in period costumes and pays them to roam the village streets reciting passages from *Moby Dick*. During my five year tenure, I'd been asked by several high school seniors to call them Ishmael.

A few months had passed now since that bloody night on Staten Island. And like small pebbles stirred into a glass of water, life had settled down with the passage of time. Settled down, certainly, but never the same.

Just after getting out of the hospital, I went to pick up my motorcycle jacket from Detective Mickelson. We spent a few minutes doing the small talk thing and eventually started discussing books we had read. He said he didn't see the value in dragging any peripheral characters into the case as long as I would testify that Robby "the Boot" had admitted killing Azrael. I said I would. And while I was at it, I suggested the late don might also have been responsible for Officer O'Toole's demise. I couldn't be certain, of course. Detective Mickelson didn't like that suggestion so well. Too tidy. Too neat. But he felt it likely

that he'd end up closing the enquiry into O'Toole's depar-
ture with a similar conclusion. His superiors, it seemed,
rather liked neatness. Mickelson's parting words were
words of warning.

"Next time I catch you impersonating an officer or
withholding evidence, we'll be discussing books from op-
posite sides of a cell door. Now get out of here."

Since I was in collection mode, I stopped off at the
Whaler on my way home from Mickelson's. When I
walked into Ben Vandermeer's office, an expression ripe
with mixed messages crossed his face like a tidal wave. He
stood up, shook my hand and sent his small staff out on
urgent errands that could have waited until the next lunar
eclipse. As the front door clicked closed, he pressed the
safe deposit box key into my palm.

"She's gone, you know."

"No, Ben, I didn't."

"Friend a mine runs a little local rag outside Phoenix.
He took her on as a favor to me."

I smiled at the irony of her job location. We both knew
she would never last.

"I made a fool of myself, Dylan," fine tears peeked at
me from the corners of his dull eyes.

"If you're gonna make a fool of yourself, Ben, love's as
good a reason as any. She got to me, too, in her way," I
admitted for the first and last time.

"She's probably laughing herself silly over what an old
fool I am."

"I don't think she's laughing at anything, Ben."

I left on that note. I liked that Vandermeer hadn't made
excuses nor had he asked me to excuse him.

With MacClough's permission and the assistance of
Mickelson and Feld, I got the state to turn Azrael's remains
over to me. The next day, John ducked out of the hospital
for the burial. I'd like to say it was a beautiful ceremony,
but I'd be lying. The weather conditions were fine if you
enjoyed gusts out of the northeast and freezing rain. Due

to the rushed nature of things, I was forced to scrounge up the rabbi who'd presided over my bar mitzvah. He was a sanctimonious prick then and after a quarter of a century he was still a prick, only an older and more expensive one. As I paid him a flat fee, Rabbi Stern completed the service in less time than it takes to soft boil an egg. But given the atmospheric conditions and Johnny's poor health, the rabbi's minute waltz best served the living.

On the road back to the hospital, I asked MacClough if he had reconsidered his decision about Azrael's daughter. He said he hadn't. I dropped the subject and started making mental plans of how I'd get her Dante Gandolfo's money and her mother's diamond heart. After some time had elapsed, I asked MacClough why he'd taken so long to act.

"I never for one minute thought it was the son," Johnny mumbled into the sleeve of his gray suit jacket. "I knew he'd loved Azrael and though I couldn't be sure, I suspected he must've known about the baby. Azrael would have gotten a message to him somehow. She was just like that. But," the ex-detective now looked away from his sleeve and to me, "if it wasn't Dante, then who?"

"How'd you—"

"The hundred grand," MacClough cut me off. "Sicilians are tighter with money than Scrooge. If it had been anyone else in the organization, Dante Gandolfo would have pushed a button on him like that." Johnny snapped his fingers. "But when the son was willing to risk that much bread to put up a smoke screen, I knew it had to be the old man. Instead of confusing things, it was like painting a bull's-eye on the old man's back.

"Unconsciously," I played Freud, "maybe that's exactly what he wanted to do."

"You worry about his unconscious. I'm too tired to worry."

I hired Bob Baum, a lawyer I'd done insurance work for. We came up with an inheritance story to facilitate passing the tenth of a million over to Azrael's daughter. Bob thought it was a cute idea, but said we could have told her anything. "Large sums of cash," he said, "tend to make instant believers out of the recipients." I could see that. But I thought the inheritance routine was a nice touch and it made turning over Azrael's heart special. I made certain that Leyna would only receive one-third of the cash up front and that she would have to petition Baum, actually me, for the second third. None of us knew her and I didn't think it was MacClough's intention to finance binges in Atlantic City. The remainder of the money was put into a trust fund for the son.

I had considered using Larry Feld to handle what I'd hired Baum for, but I still didn't trust his rebirth as a considerate human being. Familiar with his previous allegiance to self-interest and the Gandolfos, I couldn't risk his getting bopped on the head and rediscovering his lean and hungry self. I did however ask Larry to make sure Leyna Brimmer's husband didn't harass her. He didn't bother asking me how he was supposed to do that.

My short story about the Japanese visitors got finished somewhere in between the settling pebbles. *East End Monthly* had accepted it for publication and was scheduled to run the story in July. They paid pretty well, and I was fairly pleased that my relatives would finally be able to read a bit of my work in a publication somewhat more available than *Pravda*. I even had the gall to start calling myself a writer, though I wasn't at the point of having cards printed attesting to that fact.

The only writing I'd done lately was in letter form. Every afternoon since the Little League parade, I'd been hauling my ass and pad and pen into the Scupper. Mac-Clough and I would share a round and one of us would pump a few quarters into the jukebox. I played "Crazy" once, by accident, but Johnny just let it go. He'd been doing a lot of that lately. Letting go, I mean. After our drink, he'd head out back to change a keg and I'd retire to a dark table where I'd work on my letter to Marie Antoinette Gilbeau.

Confessing my guilt was the easy part. Making sense of the events since Christmas Eve was not. After failing at several attempts to explain things away with a factual recounting, I described Dugan's Dump to my Cajun pen pal. I concluded that our lives were a lot like the houses in Dugan's Dump. We're, most of us, born into a world of bright dreams and clipper ships, but those dreams often dim, forcing us to build lonely rafts out of once proud ships. I hoped that she would understand.